The Heartbreak Messenger

Alexander Vance

FEIWEL AND FRIENDS

NEW YORK

A Feiwel and Friends Book
An Imprint of Macmillan

Feiwel and Friends books may be purchased for business or promotional
use. For information on bulk purchases, please contact the Macmillan
Corporate and Premium Sales Department at (800) 221-7945 x5442 or by
e-mail at specialmarkets@macmillan.com.

Library of Congress Cataloging-in-Publication Data Available

ISBN: 978-1-250-02969-0 (hardcover)/978-1-250-04243-9 (ebook)

Book design by Ashley Halsey

Feiwel and Friends logo designed by Filomena Tuosto

First Edition: 2013

10 9 8 7 6 5 4 3 2 1

mackids.com

For Jessica, who said she would be the least-complicated person in my life.

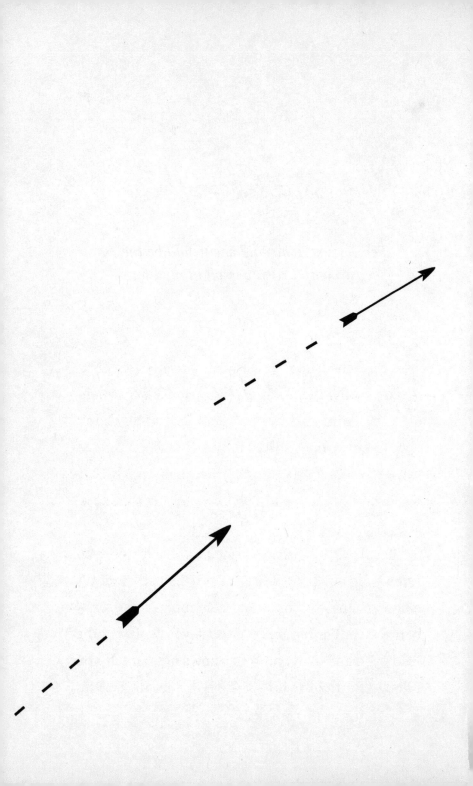

Chapter 1

I didn't choose to be the Heartbreak Messenger. Not really. I was just trying to make a few honest bucks and help a guy out. I definitely didn't choose the name. I don't know who did. It just started floating around and eventually stuck. Me? I would've gone for something more professional and less . . . girly.

Speaking of girls, I should probably tell you something about myself right off the bat—and it's embarrassing, so you can pretty much count on it being true. I'm not exactly what you would call a "ladies' man." Anyone who knows me can tell you I don't talk to girls if I can help it. I mean, besides my friend Abby and the occasional cashier at the grocery store. I'm only saying this so you'll believe me when I tell you that I didn't get involved in all this as a way to meet girls. And, for the record, I don't enjoy making people cry, either.

But, believe it or not, there are guys out there that have even more trouble with girls than I do. The crazy part is that some of those guys have girlfriends.

And that's where I come in.

It all started with Rob McFallen's older brother, who was a junior in high school. We were sitting in Rob's kitchen one afternoon eating ice cream. That was the great thing about Rob's house—both of his parents worked, and their freezer was always stocked with ice cream. As long as the rest of the house was in one piece when they came home, his parents didn't really care if half a carton of rocky road was missing.

Rob's brother, Marcus, came in and pulled out the mint fudge brownie. He had on his red delivery uniform, but he didn't seem to be in a hurry to get to work. He sat down and dug in with a serving spoon.

Rob looked up from making patterns in his ice cream with his fork prongs. "Dude, Marcus, use a bowl."

Rob had been my friend since the second grade when he'd dared me to kiss a particular girl on the playground. I didn't have the guts, so I started a fight with him instead. He finished it by throwing sand in my face. Sitting in the principal's office afterward, me blind and him busted, had bonded us for life in a prisoner-of-war kind of way. I guess you could say he was my best friend. One of two.

Marcus scowled at his brother. "Don't bug me. I'm thinking."

"First time for everything," Rob said.

Marcus didn't respond. He just sat there, staring at the spotted green ice cream on his spoon.

"Man . . . you really are thinking," Rob said.

I was kind of amazed, too.

Marcus dropped his spoon back into the carton without taking a bite. He pushed the ice cream away. "I've got problems."

I licked the dripping ice cream from my spoon. "What kind of problems?"

Rob answered for him. "Girl problems. With Marcus, it's always girl problems."

"But I thought you already have a girlfriend," I said.

"Sure, man. But that's when the real problems start." Marcus looked at me with troubled eyes.

Rob had already lost interest and was digging the marshmallows out of his ice cream. But I was curious. "Like what?"

"Like, on Monday when I picked her up for school. I wore my cross-trainers, but she made me go back home and change into my dress shoes. She said they went better with my shirt."

"Oh."

"Or Tuesday, I was gonna hang out with the guys, but she needed me to come decorate some preschool for their fall party. She wanted me to stay for the party, too! I barely escaped. Told her I wasn't feeling well."

Now *I* was losing interest.

"Or today, in English, when she saw me passing notes back and forth with Cammie Bollinger. It didn't mean nothing, but Melissa spends the rest of the day giving me the silent treatment."

"Uh-huh."

"Man, I just don't feel *free* anymore. I can't do what I wanna do. I'm trapped. I think . . . I think I need to break up with her."

Rob suddenly surfaced from his bowl of ice cream. "Break up with Melissa? But I thought you liked her."

Marcus reached across the table and swatted Rob on the side of the head. "You're so dense. Haven't you been listening? I'm miserable. I want my freedom."

"So break up with her," I said between spoonfuls.

"I . . . I'm not sure how. I've never done it before."

"Yeah," Rob said. "Girls usually dump *him*." He ducked just in time to miss another swat from Marcus's hand.

"Why don't you just send her an e-mail?" I suggested. "Or a text."

"Not a chance," Marcus said. "Tony Seong sent this sappy text to break up with his girl last year, and you know what happened? She forwarded it to everyone on her contact list, and then posted it on her blog. You can Google Tony's name right now and his breakup text pops right to the top."

"Don't be a wuss," Rob said. "Just talk to her."

Marcus glared at him. "If it's so easy, then you do it." He paused for a moment, and I saw the wheels in his head start moving again. "Hey, that's it. Why don't *you* break up with her for me?"

Rob almost snorted an almond. "What? You're crazy. Besides, Mom and Dad grounded my cell phone after I downloaded all those games, remember?"

"No, no, I mean talk with her in person. I'm serious. Go and let her know that it just isn't working out between us. That I think we should go our separate ways."

"Not a chance," Rob said. "That's so totally not going to happen."

"Please?" begged Marcus. "I'll give you twenty bucks if you do it."

My ears perked up. Twenty dollars just for delivering a message?

Rob shook his head. "Not gonna happen."

I cleared my throat. "I'll do it."

I was kind of surprised to hear myself say that.

This was probably a family thing, and I shouldn't have butted in. But I'm not one to turn down easy money. Like one year in elementary school we had a fundraiser where we had to get people to buy things from a Christmas catalog—picture frames and little angel statues and smelly decorations. The kid that sold the most would win fifty bucks. Most of the kids went door-to-door, hitting up the parents of the other kids that were selling. I figured out a better strategy. My mom knew a lady in charge of an old folk's home that let me bring my catalog there. Yeah, in one afternoon I easily claimed that fifty dollars and made a whole building full of grandmas happy at the same time.

Marcus looked at me with a hopeful half smile. "You serious?"

"Sure, if you want me to." I shrugged. "For the twenty, of course. In advance."

Marcus grabbed the ice cream carton and dug in. "Quentin, you're a lifesaver."

Chapter 2

"Seriously, Quentin, what do you know about breaking up with high school girls?" Rob asked me later that afternoon as we walked down to Mick's. "You're in seventh grade."

"Age matters not," I said in my best Yoda voice. "No . . . no."

"Yoda didn't say that. He said, 'Size matters not.'"

"No way. It was when he was talking about being nine hundred years old or something."

" 'Size matters not.' It was when Luke was trying to carry Yoda on his shoulders."

Rob and I passed the glass doors that opened

into the front of Mickelson's Quality Service Garage. It's the only auto garage in the county that's open until midnight. Plus they give you a complimentary pine-scented air freshener with each oil change. The poster in the window says WHILE SUPPLIES LAST, but Mick got a smoking good deal on half a warehouse of those air fresheners on eBay. I've seen the boxes in the storeroom and, believe me, supplies will last a good long while.

We turned the corner of the building and walked around back where the four garage bays opened up into a cement parking lot. Next to the office door in the first bay stood a chubby man in green coveralls and a red Cardinals baseball cap. As always, he chewed on half a cigar. Unlit, of course, because only an idiot would light up in a garage. Besides, he'd quit smoking years ago.

"Hey, Mick," I said as we walked past.

He looked up from his clipboard. "Quentin, my man, how's it going?" He glanced behind me at Rob. "And . . . Richard. Always welcome at Mickelson's Garage."

Rob scowled and followed me past Mick to bay four. There was an old Chevy Malibu up on the lift. Looked like an inline fuel filter job. The woman underneath it was also dressed in green coveralls. Her plain brown hair was pulled up in a ponytail and threaded through the back of a white baseball cap that didn't have a logo on it. Just grease. She looked both young and old—thirty-two to be exact—and she handled the wrench in her hand like a pro.

"Hi, Mom," I said.

She stopped cranking the wrench just long enough to look over and give me a piece of a smile. "Hey, Quentin. Hi, Rob. How was school?"

"Okay," I said.

"Guess what Quentin's going to do for my brother?" Rob blurted out.

I jabbed my elbow in his ribs before Mom looked over at us again.

"What's that?"

I shrugged. "Nothing. Just help him with some school stuff."

Mom turned back to the underside of the car and I pulled Rob across the parking lot to an old picnic table resting in the shade of a grove of poplars. The trees went out for at least a hundred yards on town land. A dirt path cut through the trees, crossing a wooden bridge on its way.

Rob rubbed his chest. "I think you cracked a rib."

"That's not something my mom needs to hear about," I said, pulling notebooks from my backpack.

"Sorry. It's not like you're doing something illegal."

"What are you doing that's not illegal?" said a familiar voice.

Abby stepped out from the poplar path and joined us at the picnic table. Her soft blond hair fell past her shoulders and a single dimple stuck in her cheek as if a thumbtack held it there.

Back in the second grade, when Rob and I got in that scuffle over daring me to kiss a girl, well, Abby was the girl. Somehow that had endeared us to her, and we'd been friends ever since. She was also my best friend, the other one of two.

"Hi, Abby. Quentin's going to . . ." Rob stopped short and looked over at me, his eyes begging me to let him go on.

I stepped in before Rob could stick his foot in

his mouth. "Nothing. Not really. I'm just helping Marcus with something. Something he wants to do for . . . or actually with . . . um, Melissa."

Abby's eyes suddenly became a brighter shade of blue. "Oh, that's so sweet of him. Like a surprise date? Or a birthday party?"

I cleared my throat. "Well, I can't really talk about it. It's kinda hush-hush."

"Quentin, come on, just give me a hint."

"I can't."

"Don't make me ask you three questions."

"Don't you mean twenty questions?" I corrected.

"No. Just three. I saw this courtroom show the other night where the lawyer was explaining how you could get to the bottom of any case with just three questions . . . if you know the right questions to ask." Everyone knows that Abby's life plan includes a successful career as a district attorney. "So are you going to tell me, or are you going to make me ask the questions?"

"I really can't, Abby. Because . . ." I hesitated. I never kept anything from her or Rob. But somehow this seemed like a good exception. I wasn't sure what she'd think about my little job for Marcus. "Because we have that grammar test on Friday that's going to kick your trash if we don't get busy."

Abby groaned and plopped down at the picnic table. "That's a hopeless cause. Why bother?"

Because it just saved me from spilling the beans, that's why. "Come on, open up," I said.

Abby and Rob dug out their books. The three of us were in several classes together, which made homework a lot easier. Abby was really good with the math and science stuff. I had English and history in the bag. And Rob . . . well, he was there for moral support.

"You want to start with number one, Abby?" I asked.

"Okay." She studied the page in her notebook. "Number one. Determine the adverb in this sentence. 'Abby was dying to know what Quentin was secretly doing for Marcus and Melissa.'"

"Abby!"

"No," she replied with a straight face. "In this case 'Abby' is a noun."

Rob snickered.

"Okay, Rob," I said without looking up, "why don't you take the first one for us?"

"Please," Abby said before Rob could respond. "Just tell me, is it romantic sweet, or fun sweet, or a help-you-out-because-I-love-you sweet?"

I snapped my notebook shut. "I'm not going to tell you. It's between me and Marcus. Just drop it, all right?"

Abby folded her arms. "Guys have no sense of romance. Fine, keep your secret. You know I'll just get Rob to tell me later."

I eyed Rob fiercely. "He wouldn't dare."

"I wouldn't?" he said.

I shook my head more confidently than I felt. "You wouldn't because I know a few things about you I'm sure you don't want shared."

Rob's eyes widened and I knew my secret was safe with him.

"Embarrassing secrets will keep you from getting elected to public office, you know," Abby said. "That's why you should never do anything you might be ashamed of later. Your past has got to be clean."

"Like you?" I asked.

"That's right," she said in a dignified voice.

I couldn't help myself. I jumped onto the table and cupped my hands to my mouth. "Hey, everybody! Abigail Patch sleeps with a Hello Kitty doll!"

Abby scrambled up onto the table and clamped her hand around my mouth. "That's not the secret I was talking about," she hissed. Her lips were tight but her eyes were laughing.

"Humppffht," I said through her hand.

"What?"

"Humppffht."

"If I take my hand off your face will you behave yourself?"

I nodded.

She slowly removed her hand. I grinned. We both stepped off the table and sat on the benches.

"Do you really sleep with a Hello Kitty doll?" Rob asked.

Abby stuck her tongue out at him.

I threw back my head and shouted, "And she has a pink unicorn night-light!"

Abby slapped the side of my arm. "You promised to behave yourself."

"I'm behaving just like myself," I laughed.

Abby gathered her books. "Then I hope you behave like someone with better manners at the show tomorrow night. You guys are coming, right?"

"Yep," Rob said.

"Wouldn't miss it," I added.

Abby swung herself out from the table. "Okay. Good. I think I'm going to head early to art club. I'll see you tomorrow." I watched her as she passed the garages and headed for the street.

She had said I might be ashamed of my secrets later. But there was nothing to be ashamed of in helping Marcus. No one would ever find out about it anyway.

"So when you gonna do the deed?" Rob asked, as if reading my mind.

I touched the twenty-dollar bill in my pocket. "Tomorrow. After school."

Chapter 3

I stood in the parking lot of the Burger Joint for a few minutes, surveying the situation. There weren't any cars pulled up to the drive-in spots. The picnic tables were also empty. There was only one customer inside. And the air was fat with the mouthwatering scent of burger grease. It was like the place was waiting for me.

You can find the usual fast-food stops in our town: McDonald's and Taco Bell and whatnot. Rob's brother delivered Chinese food for the Golden Wok, which is good. But for a real treat you go down to Fifth and Main to the Burger Joint. The Burger Joint has a sit-down restaurant on the inside, white picnic tables with large orange umbrellas on the outside, and a row of parking spaces with intercom boxes you can order from. They serve the French fries in big wedges with plenty of salt, and they stick an oversized toothpick through the middle of your burger. They even used to have the waitresses sailing around on roller skates like back in the good old days, but after one of the new waitresses lost control and took out a grandma with a walker, they did away with the skates. Which is a shame.

I'd eat at the Burger Joint every day if I could, but Mom works as a mechanic and my dad's been out of the picture since pretty much forever, so it's not like we're rolling in money. We don't go there very often. Mom calls it a "splurge" and saves it for special occasions, like birthdays or the end of the school year or stuff. But the day after I made the deal with Marcus, I headed down there right when school let out. Melissa was a waitress and I wanted to get the job over with before the afternoon customers started coming in.

I spotted her in the restaurant through a window. She and another waitress filled ketchup bottles behind a counter.

Right away my hands started to sweat. My heart beat like a bongo. I hoped that my face wasn't getting splotchy, which sometimes happens when I get nervous. Or embarrassed. Or when I eat walnuts. *Easy, Quentin,* I told myself. *You're just delivering a message. That's all. You're not talking to a girl. You're speaking for your client.*

Both waitresses had their backs turned as I walked up to the white picnic tables. I figured Melissa would like as much privacy as possible when I delivered the message, so I moved to the table farthest from the building. I sat down and tried to look casual.

A waitress spotted me and came out of the restaurant, a paper menu in one hand. She wasn't Melissa. She looked as old as my mom, with her hair tied up and tucked under her cap and white sneakers on her feet. She walked all the way to my end of the picnic area and slapped the menu down on the table. "What'll it be for you?" she asked.

My hand only shook a little as I reached for the menu. "Um . . . actually I was hoping I could see Melissa."

The waitress smirked. "Oh. I see."

Not likely. She turned and walked back into the restaurant. I brought the menu up and peeked over the top. She was talking to Melissa, pointing toward me. Melissa nodded and headed out the door.

As she came closer, my mouth went dry. It felt like my tongue had turned into a gym sock. But I timed it perfectly so that I looked up from the menu just as she arrived.

She smiled at me, a cute smile, one you might flash at a three-year-old. "I know you," she said. "You're one of Robbie McFallen's friends."

I nodded smoothly. "Yeah, that's me."

She pulled out her order notepad. "So what can I get you?"

I cleared my throat. "Actually I was hoping I could talk to you for a few minutes." I pointed to the bench on the other side of the table.

She dropped her smile. "I'm kinda working right now."

"You really need to hear what I have to tell you."

Melissa studied me for a minute, shot a glance

at the restaurant window, and stepped closer. She didn't sit down. "Make it quick."

Here was my chance. All I needed to do was say the line, pat her on the shoulder, and walk away, twenty dollars richer. But as she locked eyes with me—hers deep brown with a raised eyebrow—my mouth just couldn't form the words. So I stalled. Small talk.

"So how long have you been working here?" I asked.

That seemed to throw her off, and she relaxed a little. "Almost a year. Are you looking for a job?"

"No, not really." So much for small talk. There was only one other thing I knew about Melissa, and I figured it might point us in the right direction. "And, uh, how long have you been dating Marcus McFallen?"

Now she looked confused. "Seven months and two weeks. Why? What is this about?"

Seven months and two weeks! Marcus had been dating this girl for over half a year and was now sending someone else to end it. *What a jerk.* I pushed the thought from my mind. *Focus.*

I took a deep breath. "Melissa, I have some bad news."

Her face flooded with concern. "Has something happened to Marcus?"

"Marcus is breaking up with you." The sentence jumped out of my mouth on its own, which was good, because I didn't think I could have said it otherwise. The guilt was starting to get to me.

Melissa stared at me for a full minute. Then she sank into the bench across from me. "He sent you to tell me that?"

I nodded slowly, trying to look sympathetic. To be honest, I was expecting more of a reaction from her. Tears, for example. Or at least angry fists shaking curses to the sky and Marcus McFallen. Her eyes weren't even moist.

In fact, she laughed. A hard laugh that was lemon sour in the middle. "I love Marcus, but who knows why. That boy has no backbone." She put her elbows on the table and placed her chin in her hands. "I just can't believe that he . . . well, no, I can believe that, too."

The guilt quickly drained away, making a sucking sound in my ears like the last of the bathtub water. That had been a lot easier than I'd expected. I'd found a private setting, I'd given her the message without tripping over my tongue, and she didn't even need to cry on my shoulder.

She suddenly looked up at me. "Did he pay you to do this?"

I also hadn't expected *that*. I opened my mouth, but no sound came out. How was I supposed to respond?

She saved me the trouble. Shaking her head, she said, "Well, at least he was willing to cough up some money for me. Must have been worth it to him."

Melissa stood. She straightened her apron and pulled out her order pad and pencil. For a moment I thought she was going to ask me for my order, like nothing had happened. Instead she said, "Here's some free advice for you, little messenger. Someday, if you break up with a girl of your own, you're going to want to use flowers and chocolates. Flowers at least say, 'Thanks for the memories.' And chocolates, well, you don't want to leave a girl completely alone."

Then she turned and walked back into the restaurant.

Maybe I hadn't watched enough chick flicks, or maybe I had a heart of concrete. Maybe I was even more clueless about girls than I knew. I think most other people would have watched her walk away and felt a little pang of remorse, or at least felt sorry for her. But she'd taken it so well that I didn't feel any of that. Instead I thought about her free advice. My mind started working like a mechanic welding together a new differential case. The next time I break up with a girl . . . flowers . . . chocolates . . .

Twenty dollars in my pocket.

I wasn't sure how—yet—but this had some real potential.

Chapter 4

I thought about ordering a burger right there at the Burger Joint, since they do have the best hamburgers around. But I didn't want to call out the other waitress again, and I sure couldn't order from Melissa. Instead, I hiked down to McDonald's and got a Big Mac and three cheeseburgers, to go. And an order of large fries. I had money to burn, after all. Then I made my way over to Mick's where I knew Mom would still be cranking away. It wasn't dinnertime yet, but a hot burger early was better than a cold burger on time.

Mom's been a mechanic for years, having grown up with five car-crazy brothers. She was getting paid to work in a garage even before she graduated from high school, and even after she and Dad got married. But when I was born, she quit. She could have gotten someone to watch me, but she said she didn't want to come home to her baby with her hands smelling like grease and her fingernails looking like charcoal crescent moons.

But when Dad up and left, she put her coveralls on and headed back to the garage. Mick offered her a good salary and all the hours she wanted if she would work the night shift. She didn't like the idea of leaving me alone for so long in the evening, but we worked it out. Like garage bay dinners, for example.

I strolled into the bay where Mom was working on a Subaru up on a hydraulic lift. Looked like a muffler problem. "Hey, Mom. I brought dinner."

She stuck her head out around the edge of the car. "You brought dinner? What for? We've got stuff in the freezer."

I walked over to the little table in the corner of the bay and laid down a fresh sheet of newspaper. The comics section. I brought out the burgers and the large carton of fries, stacked up the ketch-up packets, and placed a napkin on each side of the table.

Mom was still under the Subaru, so I stepped into the empty garage office and used the office phone to dial Marcus's cell.

"Marcus," he said after two rings.

"This is Quentin. It's done."

"How'd she take it?" he asked eagerly.

"Well, she didn't cry."

"She didn't? That's good, right?"

"Uh, sure," I said.

"Thanks, man. You saved my life."

I hung up the phone and went back out to our dinner table in the garage bay. Marcus was happy, Melissa wasn't crying, and I was eating cheeseburgers. Not bad for a day's work.

Mom finally got to a stopping point and came out from under the car. She turned to the sink next to the table and filled her grimy hands full of orange-scented pumice soap. She glanced over at the table. "What's the occasion? And where'd you get the money for that feast?"

"You don't need an occasion to eat hamburgers. And I told you before that Rob's brother is paying me to help him out with some stuff."

"I don't remember you mentioning getting paid." She gave me a glance from her mom-eyes. "You're not doing his homework for him, are you?"

I laughed. "Mom, he's a junior in high school. I'm thirteen."

She scrubbed hard under the running water. "Yes, but it's Marcus McFallen. Even in his high school classes you could pull better grades than he does."

"I just thought you might like something besides microwave burritos for dinner. But I can eat yours, too, if you don't want it."

Mom wiped her hands on a shop towel and ruffled my hair with her charcoal crescent fingernails. "Thanks for thinking of me." She sat down in front of the Big Mac. "Who's turn today?"

"Yours. I picked 'human cloning' yesterday."

"That's right." She thought for a moment. "Let's go with . . . chocolate bars."

"Butterfinger," I said, my mouth half-full of

cheeseburger. "That's my favorite. Yours is the plain old Hershey's bar, right?"

"Yep."

"I've heard, though, that American chocolate is waxy. You have to taste European chocolate to get the real chocolate experience."

"Where'd you hear that?"

"Don't know. On TV maybe."

"Hmmph." Mom looked thoughtful. "I wonder why that is. Don't cocoa beans come from South America? Why don't South Americans have the best chocolate?"

"And we're closer to South America than Europe is. So you'd think that our chocolate would at least be better than Europe's."

"Well," said Mom, "we'll have to find an imports store some time and experiment."

Then we chewed in silence for a moment. But only for a moment.

When Dad left and Mom started working, we didn't have a lot of time to spend together in the evenings. Mom didn't want to waste our time together by eating in silence or getting one-word responses about my school day. So we came up with the Garage Bay Dinner Conversation game. Just two rules: take turns picking the topic, and everybody has to participate. Some topics work out better than others, but mostly we get to laugh a lot and talk a lot, which is probably more than most families do with their plates in front of the TV.

"Why is a plain Hershey's bar your favorite?" I asked. "I mean, there's no peanuts, no caramel, no crunchies. Just chocolate."

"Waxy chocolate, apparently." She winked at me. "You really want to know?"

I nodded.

"It was actually your Uncle Ethan's favorite candy bar. I don't know why it was his favorite. He just likes plain things. But when he was in the Navy, I'd send him a big package of Hershey's bars twice a month. He'd keep them in his foot-locker and make them last until the next package came. He liked his Hershey's bars, and I liked sending them.

"But Ethan noticed that someone was getting into his footlocker and eating his chocolate. He couldn't figure out who it was, and he didn't want to make a big announcement about it. So he wrote to me and had me get a bunch of chocolate ex-lax bars for him. Then I took the wrappers off the Hershey's bars and wrapped them around the ex-lax bars."

"What's ex-lax?" I asked.

"It's a medicine that makes you poop. It looks and tastes just like chocolate."

I laughed. What would they think of next?

"Anyway," she continued, "I wrapped up the ex-lax so they looked like Hershey's bars and sent them off like I always did. Ethan later wrote and said two of his shipmates spent three days in the head before they finally figured out what had happened to them."

By then I was laughing so hard I couldn't swallow my fries. Mom laughed, too.

"So when I eat a Hershey's bar, I think of Ethan. I guess that's why I like them."

I paused in my laughing to take a breath. "So do they still sell chocolate ex-lax?"

Mom gave me a warning look. "I'm not going to answer that. By the way, Abby called to remind you of her art show tonight."

"Like she's given me a chance to forget in the past two weeks," I said as I crumpled up my burger wrappings.

"It seems like she's always so busy," Mom said. "I'm surprised she has time to do everything."

"Yeah, that's Abby."

"Does she hang out with anyone besides you and Rob?"

"What do you mean? We're her best friends. Why would she want to hang out with anyone besides us?"

"No, I mean, is she seeing anyone?"

I shot her a look of disbelief. "Mom! She's not even fourteen yet. Why would she be seeing anyone?"

"Just curious. I don't know when kids these days start pairing up. Abby's the ambitious type. I could see her being interested in that."

"Trust me, Mom. Nothing is further from her mind. All she's thought about for six weeks now is the art show. And if I don't get going, I'm going to be late. Then I won't hear the end of that for another six weeks."

I tossed my trash and hit the sidewalk. Even as

I heard the clanking of tools in the garage bay echo across the street, I couldn't help but wonder why Mom was asking those kinds of questions about my best friend. Abby going out with somebody would have been as ridiculous as me having a girlfriend. Sure, there were kids in our classes who did that, but Abby? Me? I laughed out loud. Where did Mom come up with this stuff?

I turned down Robles Drive and headed for our apartment in the cool evening air.

Chapter 5

I found the only button-up shirt I owned under my bed. It was a little wrinkly, but it smelled okay, so I put it on. Rob met me out on the sidewalk. He wore slacks, a collared shirt, and a navy blue bow tie.

"What's with the tie?" I asked. "Abby didn't say anything about wearing a tie, did she?" She had given Rob and me specific instructions for the event, right down to what we were supposed to wear.

"No. But I told Marcus I was going to a cultural event and he let me wear it. I tried to talk him into letting me wear the shiny vest that matches it, but he said I already looked like a geek."

"Sounds like good brotherly advice."

Rob fingered the bow tie. "Do you think it's too much?"

"Rob, you're asking me about clothes? I'm not even sure if I wore matching socks yesterday."

"Yeah, I don't think you did."

As we headed down the street, Rob quietly pulled the bow tie from his collar and stuffed it into his pocket when he thought I wasn't looking. I tried not to smile.

"Hey, how'd that thing with Melissa go?" Rob asked.

"Mission accomplished. Not too many tears. You missed out on an easy twenty bucks."

Rob shrugged.

It didn't take long to walk down to the community center. It didn't take long to walk to a lot of places in our part of town, although to get to the east side was a different story. Our side of town still had a small-time feel to it: big enough that you didn't know all the kids you passed on the street, but small enough that their moms probably knew your mom. But the east side had a bunch of new subdivisions and business areas that kept growing and growing. They had opened a new middle school the year before, and filled all the nooks and crannies at the high school with portables. There were people everywhere.

"What are all these people doing here?" Rob asked. Dozens and dozens of people milled around the front lawn of the community center, shaking hands and talking. They were dressed in coats and ties or fancy gowns—and each one of them was way older than my mom. It looked like bingo night for the rich and famous.

I rubbed my hands down the front of my shirt, trying to smooth out the wrinkles. "Maybe Abby didn't tell us quite enough about what we were supposed to wear tonight."

Rob smiled as he pulled the navy blue bow tie out of his pocket and clipped it back onto his collar.

We worked our way to the front entrance, clinging to the building to make ourselves as invisible as possible.

"Are you sure we're in the right place?" Rob

asked after an older lady wearing too much make-up patted him on the head as she walked by.

"Well, isn't it usually old people that like to go to art galleries?"

"Quentin! Rob!" As we neared the front entrance, Abby hurried toward us. She wore a soft purple dress and her shoes had little heels on them. I'd never seen her wear shoes with heels on them before.

Abby grinned as she grabbed each of us by an arm. "Can you believe this? The community center got double-booked somehow. The Sixty-Five-Plus Club is having their annual social tonight, and lucky for us they loved the idea of having their social at our show. Isn't that awesome? They're expecting over two hundred guests—and they'll all see our artwork. Come on!"

Abby's energy practically shot through her fingertips into my arm. I couldn't help but smile to see her so excited. She was like a bag of microwave popcorn when she got like that. Just press START and watch her go.

We passed through the foyer and into the main hall of the community center. It wasn't a huge place—I doubted the whole Sixty-Five-Plus Club could have all fit, even if it hadn't been set up like an art gallery. Moveable half walls blocked off sections of the hall into several smaller rooms to display the artwork. People—not all of them old, I was glad to see—moved slowly between the walls. At the front of the room sat half-a-dozen refreshment tables stacked full of sugar, fat, frosting, and whatever the other food groups are. They were like heavy cargo ships ripe for plunder.

Abby squeezed our arms. "Remember, you promised to behave yourselves tonight. Act like gentlemen and at least pretend to be interested in the artwork. And don't go crazy on the food—there's going to be a lot of people here. Oh, Quentin . . ."

She reached up and flattened my collar out. "Couldn't you have at least ironed your shirt?" She said it with a half smile, like she already knew the answer.

"Are you kidding me?" I said. "I have a really good memory and you said nothing about ironing."

Abby rolled her eyes and gave Rob the once-over. "Nice tie. You might as well get some refreshments—I know you're dying to—and then meet me over on the far side there. I need to go find somebody first."

Rob and I waited until Abby was out of arm's reach before sprinting toward the tables like gentlemen pirates.

The spread was even more impressive close-up. I doubted that the art club had that kind of budget. It made me look forward to the day I was sixty-five-plus. Rob and I sampled from several of the tables as we piled up our foam plates. We ate the goods down to an Abby-approved portion before grabbing cups of punch and heading off to look for her. As an afterthought, I grabbed an extra cup for her and balanced it between my arm and chest.

Abby waved to us from the far side of the makeshift gallery. She stood next to someone I was sure I had seen before in the hallways at school. I figured he was probably an eighth-grader. He was tall, with dark hair and thick eyebrows. He said something and laughed. Abby laughed, too.

"Hey, guys," Abby said, still smiling. "This is Justin Masterson. He's in the art club with me."

"Rob and Quentin, right?" Justin nodded in

our direction. "Abby's told me all about you two. I didn't think either of you liked art much."

His tone of voice immediately rubbed me the wrong way. I shrugged. "Who doesn't like art?"

"Yeah." Rob nodded. "I mean, I draw sometimes. Doodles. And stuff."

Justin's smile didn't move. He had very white teeth. "Cool. Then I'm sure you'll like our show." He motioned toward the nearest wall. "Do you want a tour?" He started forward without waiting for a response.

"Oh," I said, pushing one of the cups of punch toward Abby. "I got this for . . ." It was then that I realized she was already holding a drink.

Both of our eyes darted back and forth between the cups.

"Oh," Abby finally said. "Thanks. Um . . . Justin brought me some just a minute ago." She raised her eyes from the cups to look at me. "That was nice, though." Then she followed after Justin and Rob.

I looked at the two cups and the plate of goodies I was juggling in my hands. With a sigh, I balanced the plate on my forearm and took one of the cups in my free hand. I drained it in a single chug. Grape. Stacking the full cup into the empty one, I followed the group.

"We've been studying different modern art movements," Abby was explaining as I caught up. "And then we tried to copy the style of the artists we've studied."

Justin raised his hand toward the paintings on the wall. "Like this. Our Impressionist paintings." He took a deep breath, as though smelling the paint.

I looked closer at a painting of a doorway and chair. It seemed blurry, as if it had been soaked in a tub of water. "This one looks like it's a little out of focus to me."

"Guess it's time for glasses, Quentin." Abby laughed.

Justin didn't. "That's the way it's supposed to be. You know, like Monet. The French painter."

"Ah. Gotcha." I turned toward Rob and rolled my eyes. Rob snorted and stuffed a cherry tart into his mouth.

Justin motioned to the wall across from us. "These were done after studying Jackson Pollock. Abstract expressionism."

I stared at the ten paintings arranged neatly on the wall. Each one had been splattered again and again with different colors of paint. It looked more like an accident than artwork.

Rob stepped forward and poked at one of the paintings. "I didn't know you had kindergarteners in your club."

"Rob!" Abby said.

Justin ignored the comment. "This style is a lot harder than it looks to do right. I think the one here at the top is the best." He took a step to the side and lightly placed his hand on Abby's back. "Painted by a brilliant artist I know."

I had a cream-filled pastry headed toward my mouth, but it froze in midair when I saw Justin's hand make contact with the back of Abby's dress. I waited for her to swat his hand away, but she didn't. Sure, it was probably just a friendly pat on the back between artists. Or something. But I still couldn't believe she was letting him touch her. The guy was clearly an idiot. I put the pastry back on my plate.

Abby shrugged her shoulders up around her

neck and smiled her dimpled smile. "I think they're all very good."

Even then Justin kept his hand on her back. We all stood there, staring at the splattered rectangles hanging on the wall. Except for me. I tried to distract myself by calculating how much gel Justin must have used to get the wave into the front of his hair. *It's gotta be solid enough to ride a skateboard on,* I thought. Then my eyes wandered again to Justin's hand on Abby's back. Someone had to save her.

"So what's in the next room?" I blurted out.

Justin gave Abby a quick smile and a sidelong glance before pushing her gently ahead of him toward the opening between the fake walls.

"This is our Cubism room," Abby said as we passed into it. There were several other people looking at the artwork across the room.

"Cubism . . . like Picasso," I said quickly. I was tired of knowing less than the idiot.

"Very good, Quentin." Justin said it as though he were teaching an art class. "Picasso, Braque, Gris. They tried to take the world apart and put it back together in a way no one had ever seen before. Revolutionary."

The idiot had apparently memorized whole paragraphs out of his art textbook.

"Okay," Abby said quickly. "Next room."

Rob was studying the paintings on the nearest wall. "What exactly did you take apart and put back together?"

The paintings looked like a person, probably a woman, but beyond that it was all brown squares and lines to me. I read the title under one of the paintings. *Abby by the Pool.*

Abby waved us toward the adjoining room. "I think you guys will like this next one."

"Is that really a picture of you, Abby?" Rob asked.

"We needed a model for these paintings, and we managed to talk Abby into it," said Justin. "She had some great definition in her swimsuit, so she was perfect for it."

"You modeled for everyone in your swimsuit?" I probably said that louder than I needed to. I remembered the days when Abby wouldn't go down to the river in anything but shorts and a T-shirt. Last summer, to be exact.

Abby held up her hands. "No, it wasn't like that! Well, I mean, we went swimming afterward. It was a pool party, with a little painting at the beginning. Everyone was in their swimsuit."

Still, for some reason I had a hard time picturing Abby's art club gathered around staring at her as she lounged in front of the pool. I glanced over at Justin, who looked more than a little well-built in his thick sweater and slacks.

Abby's cheeks flushed pink. "Can we please move to the next room now?"

As she headed off, Justin leaned over to me. "You know, in college art courses, they use nude models for this kind of thing." He winked at me and followed Abby.

I glared at his back. For some reason, I felt like taking him apart and putting him back together in a way he hadn't seen before.

"Hey, Quentin, are you going to eat the rest of that?" Rob pointed to my plate. I handed it to him and followed Justin.

The next room took me by surprise. Instead of pictures on the walls, there were . . . things . . . around the room. An old corded telephone stretched out, holding up laundry. A pair of canvas shoes with doodles all over them. And in the center of the room, on a shallow pedestal, was a white porcelain toilet bowl—filled to the top with M&M'S.

A man and his wife were on the other side of the room, nodding and smiling, as if sharing a joke. Two ladies with white hair and shawls also wandered through the room.

"What the heck is this?" Rob asked, half a cupcake in his mouth.

"Dadaism," Justin said. "Anti-art. It made fun of all the rules that the art world lived by. There was this guy named Duchamp who turned a urinal upside down and named it *Fountain*. I wanted to try something kind of like that." He patted the shiny white toilet tank. "I call it *Candy Dish*. Pretty cool, eh? I found the toilet out at the scrap yard, and then stuffed the bowl with newspapers and cardboard so I wouldn't have to fill the whole thing with M&M'S."

Rob reached down and grabbed a handful of candy.

I stared at him. "Rob. You just took those out of a toilet bowl."

He popped a few into his mouth. "Weren't you listening? It's not a toilet bowl, it's anti-art."

Justin grinned. "Awesome, man. That's the spirit of it. Most of us in the group really got into Dadaism, but Abby says we're crazy." He slipped his arm around Abby's shoulders and gave her a squeeze. "I still think we can win her over."

After he finished speaking, Justin's hand didn't move. It just sat there, like it was superglued to Abby's arm. Again, I waited for Abby to do something, but she just glanced down at his hand, and then looked up at me, biting her lip. I felt sorry for her. She was obviously uncomfortable with this guy's paws on her, but she was too shy to say anything about it.

A voice came over the intercom, asking the art club kids to come to the front for a brief presentation.

Abby ducked out from under Justin's arm.

"Why don't you two take a look at the rest of the artwork before our presentation? It won't be very long, I promise."

As she started toward the front of the hall, Justin offered her his hand. She hesitated slightly, and then placed her hand in his. Together they disappeared into the maze of moveable walls.

My eyes stayed focused on the exit long after they passed through.

As I stood there, the two old ladies stepped up beside me to stare at Justin's candy dish commode.

"Well, I have to say, that looks like a toilet full of candy to me," said one.

"Better than a toilet full of something else," said the other.

They both cackled.

After that, I didn't really feel like looking at the other works of art. Rob went back to the refreshment tables for a refill, and I managed to find my way outside for some fresh air. After all, it was crowded in there.

I stood on the front lawn of the community center, surrounded by senior citizens flashing their dentures at one another. All I could think about was Justin standing next to Abby, laughing. And Abby standing next to Justin, laughing back with a dimple in her cheek.

I felt a little dizzy, like my stomach had just dropped a foot or two.

Must have been something in the punch.

Chapter 6

The next day I walked home from school by myself, since Abby had art club again and Rob was running an errand for his mom. The community center looked strangely empty as I passed it. Of course, that was probably because it wasn't packed with two hundred old people in ties and cuff links. But seeing it—even without the crowd—reminded me of last night, something I was trying hard not to think about.

I distracted myself by counting the number of steps between fire hydrants, and by thinking about my history paper, and about asking Mom for money for our biology field trip to the fish hatchery, and about what I was going to have for an afternoon snack.

And about why on earth had Abby worn shoes with heels last night.

Clearly, distracting myself wasn't working.

Abby had been a regular part of my life for years. I didn't have to spend a lot of time thinking about her. She was always there. One of the guys. But since the art show, every other thought was about her. Abby with her cup of punch. Abby laughing. Abby standing next to Justin with his arm around her.

My stomach knotted up.

Why did that bother me so much? Abby was my best friend. Like a sister.

That was it. *I'm kinda her protective older brother. Of course I don't want to see some guy's arm around her. Especially not an idiot supreme like Justin. Abby deserves better than that.*

I arrived home lost in thought. I let myself in, dropped my backpack on the couch, and headed to the kitchen. I started rooting around for something to eat, when I heard Mom's voice coming from her room. I hadn't noticed her car down in the parking lot, but I hadn't been looking for it, either. She usually left for work before I got home. I paused, scooping out a glob of peanut butter, to listen.

"Of course I wouldn't, Ethan. You know me better than that." Mom's voice sounded thin and frustrated. "No, that's just it. We can't afford the rent. We'll be thrown out onto the curb within a month. . . . It won't help if I'm late for work. . . . No, I appreciate your support, you know I do. . . . All right. Love you, too."

I heard the beep of the phone and then Mom's footsteps. I tried to look really interested in my sandwich making.

"Oh, hey, honey. I didn't hear you come home."

I glanced over my shoulder. She was in her coveralls and white baseball cap. I almost expect-ed to see tears running down her cheeks or some-thing. But she looked as normal as ever.

"Hey, Mom." I tried to keep my voice steady.

"You staying in this afternoon or coming by Mick's?"

"Um . . ." I tried to form a complete sentence, but my head felt fuzzy, the echoes of the overheard phone call with Uncle Ethan ricocheting in my skull. *We can't afford the rent. We'll be thrown out onto the curb within a month.*

"I'll, uh, be there in a few. I'm doing homework with Rob."

"Okay. See you there." She grabbed her keys off the hook and rushed out the door.

Mom never really talked to me about money. She always gave me a few dollars a week for pocket cash if I helped keep the apartment clean, but other than that I never paid attention to our financial situation. It's not like I was completely clueless—I knew we didn't have much. But I always assumed we had enough.

Had our landlord raised the rent?

Were we broke?

A sickly feeling settled at the bottom of my stomach as I pushed aside my unfinished peanut butter and jam. Not being able to afford rent would mean not having a place to live. We already lived in the cheapest apartment complex in town. Maybe Mom would get a second job, which would make her even more tired. Maybe *I* would need to get a job.

It was a slow walk to Mick's, as the weight of the world seemed to press a little more onto my shoulders. And then the anger started oozing out of me, like jelly from the edges of my sandwich. Anger directed toward Anthony Chinetti.

My dad.

In the seven years since he'd left, I'd never really thought about him. Or rather, I'd tried not to think about him. I'd tried so often that my mind automatically deflected thoughts that might lead in his direction. Father's Day wasn't on my personal calendar. I avoided playing Little League because someone's dad was always the coach. I'd even dropped out of Cub Scouts back in the day because my Pinewood Derby car always looked pitiful compared to the kids who had fathers with jigsaws and sanders.

It wasn't that I hated the man, or resented him, or missed him. Mom still had a photo of him somewhere, but if I allowed myself to try, I don't think I could even picture his face.

He was just a gaping hole in my life.

But as I kicked at the sidewalk on the way to Mick's, I shot angry fireballs into that gaping hole.

Taking care of the family is the father's job. The man is responsible for making sure everyone has enough to eat, that they have clothes on their backs . . .

That the rent gets paid.

Maybe it wasn't fair for me to be angry at him then, after not letting myself think about him for so long. But Anthony Chinetti hadn't exactly been playing fair when he left us, either.

I took up my place at the picnic table, but didn't even bother to open my books. I looked over at garage bay three, where Mom had started working on an old Grand Am. Shocks replacement. She looked up and waved.

I waved back. I couldn't see the worry on her face from where I sat, but I knew it was there.

It wasn't long before Rob showed up and plopped down beside me. "Dude, Quentin, you were supposed to have your homework done by now so I could copy it." He pulled a binder from his backpack, along with a bag half-full of Golden Wok fortune cookies.

"Chow mein last night?" I asked as I reached for a handful.

"No. Potstickers with meat inside. And fried rice."

"You have it tough." I broke into the cookies, tossing the paper fortunes into my backpack.

"Are you kidding? Fighting Marcus for the leftovers he brings home is no easy job. I never even get a taste of the moo shu pork. Are we waiting for Abby?"

"She's at art club."

"Oh, yeah. Hey, that Justin guy sure had his hands all over her last night, didn't he? Seems like they might be more than just art club buddies."

The thoughts that had trailed me for most of the day suddenly reappeared. I sighed and crunched another cookie. "You noticed that, too?"

Rob snorted. "Yeah. Hard not to. I mean, I hear it happens sometimes, eighth-graders hooking up with seventh-graders—"

"Should we start with English?" I dusted the paper fortunes off my folder and pulled it out of my backpack.

Rob glanced at me. "Um, sure." He flipped open a textbook. "Hey, Ricky Mitchell told me he set up a new bike jump over at Lincoln Hill Park. Says you can get some sweet air time. We should go check it out today."

"Cool," I mumbled. My bike-jumping career had consisted mostly of twisted handlebars and scraped elbows. It came to a dead stop two years before when I broke my arm down by the river. Mom told me that I'd be paying for the next broken bone out of my own pocket. Ever since then, my bike always seemed to have a flat tire whenever Rob wanted to go jump.

"Hey."

Rob and I both looked up to see a high-schooler approaching us from across the parking lot. He had on expensive shoes and a letterman jacket with the name "Jared" embroidered on the front. I recognized him from around town, but I didn't know him. And I didn't figure he wanted to discuss bike jumping.

He stopped a few yards short of the picnic table. He looked at both of us and then pointed at me with his chin. "You the guy I'm looking for?"

I was honestly clueless. "Um . . . who are you looking for?"

"The kid that . . . you know . . ." He huffed

and glanced around before dropping his voice. His creased forehead vaguely reminded me of a ticked-off bulldog. "The Heartbreak Messenger."

I'd never heard that name before, but I immediately knew what he meant. My throat got a little tight and I couldn't swallow. It hadn't occurred to me that there might be dangers associated with the job I had done for Marcus. This was probably Melissa's brother, or cousin, or a hired hit man with instructions to take me down. Ignorance was my best strategy.

"I'm not sure what you're talking about," I said in what I hoped was an innocent voice.

The guy took a step closer. "Are you the kid that broke up with Melissa Hales for Marcus McFallen?"

There was silence for a whole five seconds. Then Rob whooped. "You're famous, Quentin! Wow! The Heartbreak Messenger. You're like a cross between a superhero and a gangster."

I could have slugged him. Hard. Instead I looked as coolly as possible at the guy in the letterman. "Yeah, that's me."

He nodded his head toward the parking lot.

"I need to talk to you." He glanced nervously at Rob.

So did I. Rob shrugged and raised his eyebrows.

I followed the guy to the far edge of the parking lot, which was hedged on one side by trees. I took comfort in knowing he could only get in a few swings before Mom or Mick would see and come rescue me. That wouldn't be too bad. Probably a few days in the hospital, and the whole school hearing how my mom had saved me from a bloody beating by knocking a high-schooler on the head with a monkey wrench.

The guy glanced around as he came to a stop, apparently satisfied with where we were. I debated whether I should try to fight back, or if that would just make it worse. But I knew Rob was still watching. I clenched my fist.

"I'm Jared. I've got a few classes at school with Marcus. He told me about what you did for him. I wanna hire you."

My fear melted away like ice cream on the pavement. "Hire me?"

"Yeah," Jared said. "I, uh, I need to break up with my girl." He was staring at the ground. "I think it would be easier . . . better . . . for both of us . . . if it went through someone else."

I felt it welling up inside me. The same feeling I'd had entering the old folks' home back in the day with a stack of fundraising catalogs, a golden opportunity ready and waiting.

I nodded sagely. "You don't need to explain to me. I understand completely."

Jared half-smiled. "I figured you would."

I cleared my throat. "I'm sure Marcus told you that my rates are high, but fair. I mean, after all, you're not going to find anyone else in town that has my kind of experience doing this."

Jared folded his arms, listening.

Deep breath. "I charge a flat fee of twenty-five dollars for a basic breakup. I'll deliver the message, and give you a confirmation when it's done. But most of my clients realize it's a little cold to have someone just deliver a message in a situation like this. So I also offer a deluxe package that includes chocolates and/or flowers." I silently thanked Melissa for her parting advice, even though this probably wasn't what she had in mind.

"Chocolates and flowers?" Jared looked slightly confused. "But I'm breaking up with her."

I smiled sadly. "Of course. But the flowers kind of say 'Thanks for the memories.' And the chocolates, well, you don't want to leave the girl completely alone."

"Why not? She'll find someone else soon enough."

Think quick. Think quick. Ah. "Let me put it this way: The easier you let her down, the less likely she'll be to come after you with pepper spray."

Jared studied me for a minute and then grinned. "I like your thinking. The Heartbreak Messenger has obviously done this before."

I spread my arms out confidently, like a jeweler behind his glass case. "So what will it be?"

He reached back and pulled out his wallet. "I'll take the deluxe package."

"Great." I realized I still had my English folder and a pen in my hand. "I don't have any of my standard forms with me, but why don't you just tell me your girlfriend's name, her address, where she works, and what her favorite flower is.

The Heartbreak Messenger will take care of the rest."

I charged Jared ten dollars for the chocolates. I had bought chocolates for Mother's Day before, and I knew I could get a nice box for less than that. I wasn't sure about the flowers, though. I made a guess at fifteen dollars. The total came to fifty dollars, more than half of which was pure profit.

Any kid would have been excited about earning that kind of cash. But by the time Jared was out of sight, I was already thinking ahead. If I was going to help Mom out with our rent, I'd need more than twenty-five dollars. I figured that our rent was probably in the neighborhood of four hundred bucks. To put down half of that, it meant eight jobs like this one each month. *Whoa*. But it had to be done.

Living in the street didn't appeal to me.

Chapter 7

When school ended the next day, I bought a box of chocolates at the grocery store and then headed down the street to Pretty Bouquets, the only flower shop I knew. A little brass bell dinged as I entered. My nose was immediately attacked by the overwhelming scent of flowers and candles and potpourri.

A middle-aged woman with her hair pulled back greeted me from behind the counter. "Hello, dear. What can I do for you today?"

"Hi. I need to buy some flowers."

"I'm glad to hear that, sweetie, because that's

what we sell." She let out a high-pitched laugh. "What kind are you looking for?"

Jared had never bought flowers for his girlfriend before, so he didn't know what kind she liked. I knew I was about to show my own ignorance, but it couldn't be helped. "Well, ones that smell good, I guess."

The woman laughed again, but not as hard. "Let me ask you this: Are they for a young woman?"

I nodded. "Yeah, they're for a girl."

"How lovely. And what does the girl look like? Her complexion, her hair color?"

"I don't know."

"You don't know? How can you buy flowers for a girl if you don't even know what she looks like?"

"I didn't think that would be a requirement."

The woman seemed a little flustered. "Of course it is. The color and the species of flower should complement the girl's appearance." She paused for a moment, and then seemed to realize something. "Oh, I see. This is a blind date."

I shook my head. "I'm in the seventh grade.

I'm way too young to worry about the whole dating thing."

She stared at me for a moment. "All right then, can you tell me the occasion for giving the flowers?"

The woman was so prim and proper that I couldn't resist telling the truth, just to ruffle her feathers a little. "I'm breaking up with her."

The flower lady straightened her back slightly and stared at me some more. "You aren't dating anyone, yet you want flowers to break up with a girl. A girl you've never seen."

"Yes, ma'am."

The woman sighed. "Then I would recommend roses. They are an all-purpose flower when it comes to matters of romantic relationships."

"How much is a bouquet of roses?"

"My bouquets start at twenty-four ninety-nine."

Ouch. I pointed to some other flowers behind the counter. I thought they might have been tulips. "What about those?"

"Those bouquets start at eighteen ninety-nine."

I pointed to some others. Maybe lilies. Or orchids. Or something else.

"Fourteen ninety-nine."

My profits were evaporating before my eyes.

"What's the cheapest bouquet of flowers I can get from you?"

The lady sighed again, defeated. She handed me a bouquet of white flowers wrapped in green paper. "Carnations. Nine ninety-nine. Traditionally a funeral flower."

"Now we're talking." I paid for the flowers and the lady told me I could pick out a message card for free. I chose one that said, "My Sympathies." I didn't think the "Congratulations" card would be appropriate, although I briefly considered "Get Well Soon." I stuck the card into the center of the flowers and headed for the exit. I had a message to deliver.

I hadn't gone a block from the flower shop when my nerves began to get to me. There I was, about to meddle in somebody else's relationship. Meddle, nothing. I was going to tear it down like a trigger-happy demolition man. With Marcus and Melissa it was different. I knew them. But these were two strangers. It felt weird and exciting and terrifying all at once.

And then, as I rounded the corner of the grassy high school sports fields, I saw Abby coming toward me. Then it felt mostly terrifying. I stuck the flowers behind my back.

"Hey, Quentin," she said as we both came to a stop on the sidewalk. "What's with the flowers?"

"Flowers?" I looked into my hands as though they'd been empty seconds before. "Oh . . . those. Um, they're not for me. I mean . . . I'm not going to give them to . . . or actually . . . um, they're not from me to anyone. In particular." Smooth as silk.

"But . . . they're for a girl?" Abby asked the question slowly, like she was trying to solve one of those mind-bender puzzles and talk at the same time.

I was stuck. What the heck was I supposed to say? I couldn't make up a lie about giving the flowers to just anybody. I figured I had no choice but to tell her the truth, for better or worse.

But Abby narrowed her eyes. "Are those part of your secret with Marcus and Melissa?"

She apparently hadn't heard the latest news about that ex-couple. But I saw my way out and dove for it headfirst. "Well . . . you know I can't tell you that. But you're headed in the right direction."

An odd look of relief flooded Abby's face. "Oh, good. I mean, good for Melissa and all. Anyway . . ." She smiled at me slyly. "Are you sure you can't give me a hint about their secret?"

"I wish you'd stop asking. I already told you no." I said it more sharply than I meant to. My nerves were already on edge and my encounter with Abby wasn't helping.

"Sorry. Just curious. I could even help if you wanted me to."

"Thanks. It's not your kind of thing, though." It was time to move on. The bouquet of white flowers was somehow getting heavier by the minute.

Abby put her hands on her hips. "Not my kind of thing? Are you saying romance isn't my kind of thing?"

No, I was saying that I needed to go before I jammed my foot in my mouth any further. "Well," I said, "I wouldn't expect you to know anything about romantic relationships, because you've never had one."

"Neither have you, Mr. Romance." She was slipping into her district attorney tone of voice. Challenging me. I didn't have time for that, but my blood was getting hot. I ignored the flashing red warning lights in my head as my shields went up and I switched into defense mode.

"And I don't need one. I'm thirteen years old. Maybe when I'm ready to get married I'll start looking, but meanwhile I've got more important stuff to do with my time."

"Like what?"

Hmmm. She had me there.

"Like help Marcus out with *his* girlfriend?" Abby said.

"No, like . . . sports."

"You don't play sports."

"I do karate," I said.

"I thought you quit your karate class."

"So I'm between interests right now. What difference does that make?"

"The difference is that you don't have a girlfriend because you have no idea how to get one."

"Maybe I don't have a girlfriend because there aren't any girls around here worth looking at."

Abby stared at me without a word. The look on her face made my defense mode blow a fuse and it shut down entirely.

"Hey . . ." I said.

"Art club is at the high school today," Abby said quickly. "I gotta go. See ya." She brushed past me, leaving me with the bouquet of white flowers and the strong taste of foot on my tongue.

I sighed. Abby and I often had friendly debates about the important things in life. Stuff like vegetarianism versus the benefits of fast food; whether school money should be spent on the arts or classroom video game systems; and the age-old classic rock versus alternative argument. But this conversation had completely imploded. Something was up, and I couldn't figure out what.

I trudged up the sidewalk and headed for the soccer field, hoping to score better in the second half.

Chapter 8

An image came to mind as I sat in the bleachers at the high school soccer field with a box of chocolates and a bouquet of carnations. It was from an animal documentary on TV about the Serengeti in Africa. This group of hyenas had come across a dead wildebeest and started chowing down. One hyena decided he wasn't getting his fair share, so he laid into another hyena to get him to move. The other hyena didn't like that, and they started to fight. Before you knew it, the entire clan of hyenas was in one massive brawl with teeth, claws, and tails flying. In the end, one of the hyenas got killed and they made lunch out of him instead of the wildebeest. I guess everyone likes their food fresh.

I was watching the girls' soccer team play a scrimmage game against their second-string lineup and it looked just like that scene with the hyenas—except the grass was greener and the girls wore jerseys. I'd heard rumors that this team had the regional record for the most red cards pulled on them in a season, and by watching for just a few minutes, I could see why. There was enough shoving, slide tackling, and angry shouting to fill a WWE arena.

I searched the field for number sixteen. I found her just in time to see her drop a shoulder and plow into a player wearing a white jersey. She pointed two fingers in a victory sign as her opponent fell to the ground. That was Carmen Mendoza.

I wondered if she would take the message as coolly as Melissa had.

The game went on for a while. The white jerseys were getting creamed, although there were plenty of elbows thrown on both sides. To keep my mind off the injuries Carmen was passing around, I pulled out the notes I'd jotted down on what I was going to say to her.

Jared sent me to break up with you for him. He wants me to give you these flowers and chocolates as a parting gift. Thank you and good luck.

On the field, Carmen was yelling at a team-mate. With Melissa everything had gone so smooth-ly that I really hadn't put much thought into how this would work with someone else. My hands were sweating.

I looked at my notes again. I needed something better for a high-pressure situation like this. Like a movie script. Movies are always full of people that know exactly what to say. Even when people in movies say something dumb, it still sounds good. What I needed was a cool one-liner.

Then I remembered the fortune cookies Rob and I had scarfed the day before. I dug into my back-pack and found a few slips of paper scattered at the bottom. I unfolded the first one.

A misstep will bring you great pain. I glanced up in time to see Carmen body check an opponent. I ripped the fortune in half and pulled out another.

Love asks me no questions and gives me endless support. Nice thought, but I figured Carmen would probably have a few questions to ask Jared when this was through.

Next. *You will be invited to a karaoke party.* Good to know.

I unfolded the last paper fortune. *Saying good-bye brings such great sorrow.* Well, it wasn't exactly Oscar-winning dialogue, but given the options, I decided it would have to do.

I repeated the phrase over and over again in my mind until I had it down. I needed to be confident, yet sympathetic. Bold, yet understanding.

When the coach finally looked up from the paperback he was reading and blew hard on his whistle, I was ready. The girls grabbed their equipment and water bottles and moved toward the locker-room entrance. I maneuvered down the bleachers and trotted across the field to head them off. When I was close enough, I called, "Carmen!"

Flanked by two of her teammates, Carmen glanced in my direction, but then kept walking. I put on a little more speed and came up right in front of her. I paused a moment to catch my breath.

She stared at me with hard, dark eyes. "What do you want, punk?"

"I need to talk with you," I said. Her teammates giggled, looking at the flowers and the chocolates. "Alone."

She didn't blink. The other girls stayed beside her, laughing a little more. Carmen's forehead glistened with sweat. A droplet hung from her nose, somehow making her seem even more savage. "What do you want, little boy?"

I spoke as forcefully as I could, mostly just to keep my voice from cracking. "I have a message for you. From Jared."

That made her blink. But just once. "Well?"

I cleared my throat and held out the flowers, resisting like heck the urge to turn and run. "Saying good-bye brings such great sorrow."

Carmen batted the flowers aside and took a step closer to me. "I'm getting tired of you already, little punk. Now tell me what this is about."

I cleared my throat again and forced myself to look into her eyes. *I'm a professional. I'm a professional.* "Jared sent me to tell you that he's breaking up with you."

Carmen's dark skin flushed red, and the hard lines faded away. Her friends weren't laughing anymore. She spoke quietly. "You wanna say that to me one more time?"

Not really. I cleared my throat again. "Jared asked me to come tell you that, um, he's breaking up with you." *Steady, man.* I looked down at the items in my hands. "He wanted me to give you these as a token of his . . ."

And that's when it hit me. I don't know for sure what it was. Probably Carmen's fist, although it felt more like a rock, or maybe a can of beef stew. I went from staring at the white flowers of death to staring at a bright flash of stars to finally staring at the blue sky peppered with clouds. I found myself flat on my back in the grass, and my head was throbbing.

It was kind of a surreal moment, like the exact instant when an ordinary guy in the comic books turns into a superhero. It was as though my sense of hearing was enhanced beyond normal human abilities. I could hear the cars idling at the traffic light on the other side of the field. I could hear the feet of the cross-country team making their way around the circuit. I could hear the doors of the girls' locker room open and slam and open and slam. And, though I couldn't really be sure, I thought I heard, maybe, the sound of Carmen crying.

And that's when I passed out.

Chapter 9

I don't think I was unconscious on the soccer field for very long. When I came to, I found myself staring up at a bunch of cheerleaders who wanted me to get off the field so they could practice. They were really polite about it, though. One of the guy cheerleaders even offered to pick me up and carry me off, if I needed help.

The carnations still seemed to be in pretty good shape. They had been knocked around a little, but all the petals were still intact. And, unlike me, the box of chocolates had also made it through the incident unharmed. I took them home and actually considered myself lucky. Carmen had obviously refused the gifts—boy, had she refused the gifts—and so I had no problem with saving the merchandise for a future job. Assuming there would be another job. There were apparently some risks I'd have to think through first. Death, for example.

I pulled out a glass vase from under the sink for the flowers and put them in my room. I placed them next to the window and then piled up a big mound of clothes and junk in front of them so they didn't look so obvious. I didn't really want Mom to suddenly see a vase of flowers in her son's bedroom. She might wonder about me. I resisted the temptation to eat the chocolates by stuffing the box in my underwear drawer.

Then I dug out a bag of frozen peas from the freezer and wrapped it in a dish towel. As I held it up to the left side of my face, I had to admit that Carmen's reaction had completely taken me by surprise. I mean, I could understand her getting upset with the jerk-wad that broke up with her. But didn't she know that you don't shoot the messenger? I was sure I'd heard that in a movie. Somewhere.

The icy towel began to sting my skin, soothing

and hurting at the same time. I went into the bathroom and stared at myself in the mirror. I gently lifted the towel to reveal four different colors spreading out along my swollen cheek.

It was a shiner to be proud of.

That thought made me stand up a little straighter. I had been clobbered by the star player of the (girls') soccer team. Someone so fierce that she left a trail of broken bones and red cards in her wake. And yet I had stood up to her without flinching. Carmen Mendoza may have been tough, but the Heartbreak Messenger was a force to be reckoned with, too.

I glanced at the clock, then back at my multi-colored face. Maybe Mom wouldn't notice.

♥ ♥ ♥

At three minutes apiece, it didn't take long for me to have our microwaveable TV dinners hot and ready to go on the table at Mick's. Making dinner is so easy. I don't know why people complain about having to cook. Mom washed at the sink and sat down. She glanced at me, then down at the dinner tray, and inhaled. "Mmmm. Chicken-fried steak and creamed corn." She smiled. So far so good.

I grabbed my plastic fork and dug in. "Your turn, Mom," I said between the first and second bites.

"Let's see. How about . . . fighting at school?"

I looked up at her, trying to keep my face as straight as possible, which took some serious effort under the scrutiny of mom-eyes. "Fighting at school? I'm against it. One hundred percent. It seems to me that only a dipstick couldn't figure out a solution to a problem without resorting to throwing punches." I hoped that Carmen wasn't within earshot.

"Oh, I don't know about that," Mom said. "I suppose even intelligent guys realize that sometimes they have to fight to get what they want, or to do what's right, or to defend themselves. The difference between an intelligent guy and a bonehead is that the bonehead fights first and thinks later. The other guy thinks it through, looks at the options, and then decides that fighting's the best choice he's got."

I stopped chewing, my mouth hanging half-open. Moms aren't supposed to talk that way, even my mom, the grease monkey. Somehow, though, what she said made a lot of sense. I finally nodded my head and finished chewing. Despite her words of wisdom, I knew there was no hiding it. "Does my eye look that bad?"

"It ain't pretty."

I finished off my mini portion of cherry cobbler before saying anything else. "Well, it wasn't a fight. More of a misunderstanding. There was this guy that broke up with his girlfriend, and I happened to be standing nearby when it happened. The girl just went totally ballistic and started hitting things, including my eye."

She tried hard, but there was no way for Mom to hide a smile when it was so plain on her face. "A girl did that?"

"She was a . . . tough girl. A soccer player."

By then she was laughing. Hands-over-her-mouth laughing.

It was just my mom, but I could feel my ears turning pink. "I'm serious, Mom. They give her red cards like they're lunch tickets."

She kept going. Soon her eyes were watering.

"Mom, you're not doing much for my sense of manliness."

She forced herself to grab a breath. "I'm sorry, Quentin." She closed her eyes and took another deep breath. "Did this happen at school? Do I need to talk to the principal about it?"

My eyes got wide, including the purple one. "Are you kidding? As far as the rest of the world knows, I hit my head on the bathroom sink when I bent down to tie my shoe."

Mom reached across the table and ruffled my hair. "My poor baby."

I pulled back and grinned. "No, it's too late for that. You keep your fake pity to yourself."

As I walked home after dinner, my thoughts wandered back to the fifth grade. That year Rob got into a fight on the playground with a fourth-grader who was picking on him. To Rob's credit, it was Stubs Thompson, the biggest kid in the school who had been held back a grade—twice. But still, a fourth-grader. No one really got hurt, but they both got in plenty of trouble. I remember Rob telling me about the long talk he'd had with his dad the night after it happened. His dad had been totally cool about it. He'd shared a few stories about fights from his school days, talked about when it was okay to stand up for yourself and when to let it go, and how to hold up your left fist in front as a guard. I think he even took Rob out for ice cream or something.

I'm pretty level-headed and hadn't ever been in a fight. (Rob throwing sand in my face in the second grade didn't count.) Carmen Mendoza's fist was the first time I'd even come halfway close. Since Rob's experience, though, I'd wondered on occasion what would happen if I got into a fight. I mean, I couldn't have asked for a better reaction from my mom for that black eye. But still, talking about something so personal and manly as your first shiner—it really ought to come from a father, you know? I suppose I wasn't the first single-parent kid to feel cheated out of stuff.

Mom always says that you shouldn't waste any time feeling sorry for yourself. But as I turned down our street in the blue evening light, I reached up and gently touched the swollen skin around my left eye, and winced.

Chapter 10

Carmen Mendoza had hammered into me the idea that this Heartbreak Messenger business might be a little risky. I figured Carmen was probably an extreme case—I really hoped she was an extreme case—but it was enough to make me argue with myself about whether I should keep the business going. The seventy dollars I'd pulled in was amazingly persuasive, however, and it didn't take long for the money to win the argument. If I was going to risk my life, at least I stood to make some good money doing it.

But that presented another problem: If this gig was going to work, there had to be a steady stream of clients. Advertising was out of the question—just in case Carmen *wasn't* an extreme case. I needed a way to drum up business without announcing to the world that I was the Heartbreak Messenger and you could find me in apartment 326T.

I needed a front man, someone out in the field of potential clients who could make the sale for me. So I turned to the only high-schooler I knew.

"Marcus, I have a proposition for you," I told him one afternoon over a bowl of chocolate chip cookie dough ice cream.

"Oh, yeah? What's that?"

"You know how you told Jared about the help I gave you with Melissa?"

"Oh, sure. Man, he was hurting something bad. Problem was, he knew Carmen would beat the crud out of him if he broke up with her himself." Marcus laughed. "In fact, I haven't seen him at school since you delivered the message. He's probably still lying low, just in case."

I rubbed the side of my face, which was still a little tender. "Do you think you could find other guys that might need my services? You know, send them my way like you did Jared?"

"I'm sure I could. . . ." Marcus's eyes grew a little wider. "I see. You want me to drum up business for you. Yeah. In fact, I know a couple guys off the top of my head that might want a little help. I'll talk to them. For a cut, of course."

"How about ten percent of the profit?"

Marcus stuck out his hand. "Deal." I knew it would take him awhile to crunch the numbers and figure out it only came to two-fifty a job. In the meantime, I now had my front man.

Marcus was as good as his word. The next Monday after school, as I headed out of the junior high, Marcus was standing there with another high-schooler. Marcus pointed toward me and flashed a thumbs-up. I changed direction and headed for an empty part of the school yard. My new potential client, a tall kid with a shaved head and glasses, sauntered over.

"What's up?" he said. "I'm Ty. My man Marcus says that you're the Heartbreak Messenger."

"That's right. What can I do for you?"

The guy bit his lower lip and looked up at the sky for a good, long moment. "I gotta break up with my baby." He smoothed down his eyebrows with his fingertips.

I waited for him to go on. His eyes were getting a little moist.

"I'm no good for her, see. That's what her mama says, that's what her girlfriend says, that's what everybody says. And they're right, man." He sniffed, long and loud. "I love her, but I'm no good for her. I gotta end it."

"Oh. I'm sorry. I guess." I felt like an undertaker talking about funeral arrangements. "What's her name?"

"Her name's LaTisha. It means 'great happiness.' And that's all she's brought to me. I got a picture right here." He whipped out his wallet and flipped it open. "See?"

It was a picture of Ty and a girl with big hair making kissy faces at the camera as one of them held it out to snap the photo.

"And where can I find her?" I asked.

"She works the desk down at Chic Clinique on Fifth. She always smells like the shampoo of the week."

"Uh, right. Well, a lot of guys want me to take the girl chocolates and flowers. . . ."

"Nah, none of that. She's got allergies for, like, everything."

"Okay." In my mind I could see the carnations wilting away in my room. "Well, then . . ."

"But I do have a song."

"A what?"

"A song, man. It's our song. Hers and mine. It's something special, and I wrote it myself. I want you to sing it to her. Kind of a going-away present from me."

"Well, I'm not much of a singer. . . ." Understatement of the year. Mom actually asked me *not* to sing in the shower.

"No worries. Powerful lyrics like this sing for themselves. Poetry. It's all about what's here that counts." He thumped his heart with his fist. "It goes like this. . . ."

Every once in a while life hands you a surprise, something you never could have guessed was going to happen. A high-schooler serenading me on the junior high blacktop was one of those things.

"You see the moon, You see the star,
But me alone, I won't go far."

Ty didn't hold anything back. His voice warbled and rose up and down like he was serious stuff in a recording studio. I glanced around to see a few stragglers still leaving the school grounds. I tried to look natural, which was hard since Ty had some hand motions and arm waving to go with those powerful lyrics.

"You have my love, you are my fire,
Like the sun above, you're my desire.
Ba . . . by."

He savored the final note like it was a piece of creamy European chocolate. "You got that?"

"Um, close enough." My screechy rendition would mostly be unintelligible anyway. "Now about the money . . ."

"Oh, and there's one more thing, Heartbreaker. My ring."

"Your ring?"

"Yeah, she's got my class ring. The one with the red stone in the middle. She wears it everywhere. But since we're going our separate ways and all, I'm gonna need it back."

What did he think I was running, a singing repo service? I'd heard that the customer is always right, but after the Carmen Mendoza business, I was a little wary about getting close enough to grab a ring. "You sure you need it?"

"Yeah, man. I paid good money for that ring. Just give it to Marcus when you got it. He knows where to find me."

I charged him thirty, since love songs and ring retrieval were a little outside of my normal job description. He was cool with that, except that opening his wallet to get my cash brought LaTisha into view again, which meant an encore performance. I hummed along.

♥   ♥   ♥

Chic Clinique was just a few blocks from Mick's, so I went to the garage to drop off my things first. Rob and Abby were already at the picnic table, notebooks out.

"Hey guys," I said as I tossed my backpack onto the table. "I need to run an errand. I'll be back in a few."

Abby looked a little disappointed. I figured it was because we had an English assignment due the next day and she wanted help with it. "Don't worry," I said. "I'll be quick."

I made my way over to Chic Clinique, a small shop squeezed between an all-oak furniture store and an Army surplus outlet. I put my face up to the window to see several customers in swivel chairs, and several employees doing hair and nails and whatever else they do in places like that. None of them looked like the photo of LaTisha.

I started to turn away when I saw the receptionist desk crammed into the front corner. Behind it, reading a magazine, sat the girl who was apparently too good for Ty.

Now, how to get her alone? The thought of going inside a room full of gossipy women terrified me. Who knew what deep secrets they might be able to pry out of me with their arsenal of cosmetic chemicals. I also needed to be outside just in case any of them had grudges against guys and didn't take kindly to Ty's message.

I moved to the nearest window and tapped quietly. LaTisha didn't look up. I tapped again, a little harder. I felt a few of the hairdressers and nail filers turn in my direction, but LaTisha remained glued to her magazine. I banged on the window with my knuckles. LaTisha looked up at me, along with every other person in the salon.

Not quite the subtle approach I had planned. I smiled weakly and motioned LaTisha to come outside. She gave me a funny look, but I heard one of the other employees say something. LaTisha sighed and put her magazine down and headed for the entrance.

"Hey. What do you want?" she asked as she stuck her head out the door.

"Are you LaTisha?"

She looked a little confused. "Yeah. Who are you?"

After Carmen, I'd taken some time to look up a few good one-liners on the Internet, and I had one ready for LaTisha. Kind of an icebreaker, you know. " 'The hottest love has the coldest end.' " Socrates. Being able to toss out a saying by someone both dead and Greek makes you seem all the more professional.

"Yeah, that's nice kid. You waiting for your mom? I'm sure she'll be done soon." LaTisha started to duck back inside.

"Ty sent me."

That made her stop. "Ty?" She stepped out onto the sidewalk, the door swinging closed behind her.

I cleared my throat. "Ty sent me to tell you that he's no good for you, and he's breaking up with you."

LaTisha stood there with her mouth open, her eyes moving back and forth, as though she were trying to read the joke on my face that wasn't there.

"Why are you messing with me?" she asked, her eyes flashing between anger and desperation.

"Um, I'm not. Really. In fact, I have a song he asked me to sing." I hummed a starting note just to see how it sounded before launching into it.

"You see the moon, You see the star . . ."

LaTisha stepped forward and shoved my shoulders. "Oh, no you don't!"

I jumped clear and backed a few steps into the street, my heart in my throat. My eye was just returning to its natural color, which was how I wanted to keep it.

LaTisha stood on the curb, hands on her hips. Her head wove from side to side as she spoke. "How dare you tell me Ty's breaking up with me and then go and sing our song. That ain't right. You don't treat a woman like that. You go back and tell Ty that if he wants to break up with me, he comes and tells me himself."

"Well, actually, I'm in the business of taking messages. Maybe I could help you out." One side of my brain was screaming at me to keep my mouth shut, but the other side couldn't let a potential opportunity pass me by.

Her eyes narrowed. "If you wanna help me, you'll turn your skinny junior-high butt around and go let the air out my ex-boyfriend's tires."

There was business potential there, too, but that seemed a little more risky.

LaTisha turned, ready to take her icy storm into the Chic Clinique where it would probably become hot gossip.

"Uh, one more thing, please."

She gave me a sidelong gaze of death with one hand on the door.

"Ty wants his ring back. His class ring with the red stone in the middle."

Her look was what a vulture might give a half-dead deer on the highway before tearing into it.

She walked back toward me with a casual swagger. "He wants his ring back, does he?" She pulled a gold ring off her middle finger. "The ring I helped him pick out? The ring he told me represents his undying love for me? The ring he said he was gonna replace someday with a diamond? That ring?"

"Well, um, does it have a red stone? If it's the one with the red stone, then yes."

She held up the gold ring with the red stone in the middle. "Here you go."

I hesitated, and then took a step forward with my hand out. I could hardly believe she was really going to give it to me.

She moved her hand toward mine, dangling the ring above it. Then just before she let it go, she moved her hand to the side. The ring plunged like a skydiver without a chute down toward the street. With a metallic *clink* it hit the metal grate of the storm drain. With another *clink* it struck the second set of bars. And with a *thud* it stopped at the concrete bottom.

LaTisha lifted a single eyebrow and then slowly turned and strutted into the salon.

I stared after her, wondering if Ty had broken up with his girlfriend, or if it was the other way around.

Chapter 11

Oh, brother," I mumbled, staring into the storm drain. Water-swept leaves and grass with a sprinkling of candy bar wrappers decorated the wide crisscrosses of the first grate. The filth on the lower grate was barely recognizable. And the concrete floor on the bottom glistened with a thick green layer of who-knew-what.

I got down on my hands and knees and peered into the semi-darkness. It wasn't very deep. I could probably reach the ring if I really stretched, and if my hand could fit through the narrow openings of the second grate. The question was, did I really want to?

If I didn't return the ring to Ty, he would probably want his money back. He might even think I'd stolen the ring and sold it on the junior high black market. Or worst of all, he might start telling his friends what a botched job the Heartbreak Messenger did for him. One rumor like that spreading through the high school locker room would put a stop to my business like a brick in front of a bike jump. And I'd be left with nothing to help Mom out with the rent.

I leaned down and stuck my hand through the first grate.

I squinted and held my breath as I passed my hand through the second grate. I tried not to touch the slimy metal, but it wasn't easy, since I had to stretch my fingers out and fold my thumb in just to get it through the small opening. The built-up filth felt like wet leather on my warm skin.

Once my hand was through, I pressed my shoulder against the first grate and groped for the ring. I forced myself to run my fingers over the moist cement bottom, since it was hard to see anything down there. I thought I could make out a glint of clean metal, several inches from my fingertips. I couldn't stretch any farther, so I pulled my arm out, moved over a little, and then pushed in through the grates a second time.

The stench coming from the wide mouth of the sewer made it hard to breathe. A slight wave of nausea rolled through my stomach and I tried to think more pleasant thoughts. A hot shower and hand sanitizer, for example.

It took me a bit of feeling around, but in time I struck gold, literally. I snagged the ring with my fingertips. But as I pulled my hand back out, holding the ring like that, I found that my hand was too wide to fit through the grates. I felt the ring slipping from my fingers as I pulled.

"Quentin?"

I twisted my head around, trying to keep the rest of my body as still as possible. Abby stood above me on the sidewalk.

"What are you doing?" she asked.

"I, uh, dropped something and I'm trying to get it back out. Bad luck, eh?"

"Right." Abby shifted her weight from foot to foot as she chewed on a fingernail.

"I'll be there in a few minutes for homework.

As soon as I get finished with this." I gently tugged my hand back toward the opening in the grate, but I could feel the ring getting squeezed out from between my fingers, like a cartoon banana out of a peel.

"Hey, Quentin, I need to talk to you about something."

"Um, okay." I turned just a little so I could look at Abby without twisting my neck into a Twizzler. I mashed the ring between my fingers as tightly as I could.

Abby sat down on the curb a few feet away. Her fingers fiddled with a woven bracelet on her wrist.

"Do you remember Justin Masterson? The guy you met at the art show?" She asked her question carefully, like she was opening one of those peanut cans that have a springy snake inside.

"Yeah," I said. *Hard to forget a head as big as his.*

Abby fidgeted with her bracelet a little more, and then finally stood and started pacing in tight little circles. "Well, we know each other pretty well. I mean, we've worked on a lot of art projects together, and we've both been in the club for a while, and . . . I mean, he's seen me in a swimsuit, for crying out loud, and he's even met my mom and dad. And he's an *eighth*-grader."

Abby, hurry it up, I pleaded silently. *There is no more blood in my arm.* She seemed to be talking more to herself than to me, anyway. Then she stopped and looked down at me as she stood on the sidewalk, seeming mighty tall from where I lay with my arm in the sewer.

"Justin's asked me to be his girlfriend."

It took forever for her words to sink in, like dropping a pebble into wet mud. I felt lightheaded from the sewer smell and my brain was as numb as my arm.

By the time the sentence worked its way into my gray matter, Abby had already moved on. "I mean, I think Justin's nice and everything, and really kinda cute, but you know . . ." She took a deep breath. "I guess what I really want to know, Quentin—as my best friend, of course—can you think of any reason why I shouldn't go out with Justin?"

An hour later, I would be able to think of a million reasons.

Because he's an idiot.

Because he wears bulky sweaters to make it look like he goes to the gym twice a day.

Because he's an eighth-grader who gets his teeth whitened.

Because he swallowed an art encyclopedia and could tell you every messed-up detail about what Jackson Whosawhatsit ate for breakfast.

Because spending more time with him means spending less time with me.

But in that moment, up to my shoulder in slimy cast iron with my brain apparently in standby mode, all I could think was, *My arm's going to fall off.*

"Any reason at all?" Abby's eyes seemed to be searching for something written on my face, or hiding in my eyes. She was probably seeing the pain of a nearly dislocated shoulder.

"Not that I can think of," I said.

She just stood there, staring at me. Like I'd given her the wrong answer or something. Then she nodded her head slowly and spoke just louder than a whisper. "All right. Thanks, Quentin."

Then she turned and left.

And the ring fell with a *clink* back to the bottom of the storm drain.

Chapter 12

I couldn't figure out why Abby had come to talk to me about Justin. And I really couldn't figure out why she seemed disappointed with my answer. But I was starting to realize that there was a mysterious territory surrounding girls that even older guys seemed to get lost in. That made me feel a little better about being completely clueless.

I remember studying Egyptian hieroglyphics in my history class. Scholars had a hard time trying to figure out what they meant, until they discovered the Rosetta Stone. That was this big rock that a guy in the French army found in Egypt a few centuries ago that had the same paragraph in three different languages—including hieroglyph-ics. With that, the scholars could translate it and use it to figure out what the weird symbols meant.

I was starting to think that there should be a Rosetta Stone for girls. Something that translated what they said and did into what they really meant. Something that could help me understand how Abby and I had gone from playing tag at recess, to hanging out as best buds, to . . . what? Was I her relationship counselor now? I wasn't sure I was qualified for that.

You know that French scholar who found the Rosetta Stone and gave it a name? I'll bet his girl-friend's name was Rosetta.

After Abby left me lying empty-handed in the gutter, and the circulation returned to my finger-tips, I finally realized that I had to be smarter than the sewer grate. It only took a tree branch, three pieces of cinnamon gum, a borrowed shop light, and an hour of trying not to cuss, and that ring was out of the sewer and in my hands at last.

I sent the ring back to Ty. I didn't hear any-thing from him, so I guessed he didn't notice the green sludge packed into his graduation year. And what's more, Marcus kept sending break-up jobs my way, even though his cut wasn't huge. I kinda figured he liked being able to get in good with his buddies by pointing them in the direction of relationship relief. I had to remind him constantly about keeping my identity as secret as possible—paying customers only. But I probably stressed over nothing. While breakups are always food for high school gossip, the identity of an insignificant middle-schooler was not.

But take even the most boring high school rumor, drop it into junior high, and it'll spread like chicken pox.

I didn't usually listen much to the gossipers, but something caught my attention one day as I passed through the hall on my way to algebra. It happened so fast that I didn't even know who said it or where in the hallway they were. But I heard the words "Carmen Mendoza" and "Heartbreak Messenger" in the same sentence.

My heart stopped. I could almost feel Carmen's fist against my face, and I fought the urge to duck. As casually as possible I pulled over to a wall of lockers and looked around, ears open. Nothing. But it made me more than a little worried just the same. And, if I was being honest, just a little excited.

I finally heard the whole rumor, at least a version of it, the next day in world history. Two girls that sat behind me, Vicki and Jennifer, were queens of secondhand gossip.

"So did you hear about Carmen Mendoza on the high school soccer team?" Vicki whispered. She didn't really need to whisper. Our teacher, Mr. Hogan, *was* a piece of world history and couldn't even hear the bell most of the time. Besides, he was deep into a lecture on the Trojan War and Greek mythology, and wouldn't surface for a while.

"Yeah," Jennifer said, "about her boyfriend dumping her?"

"Well, yeah, but it wasn't even her boyfriend. He sent that Heartbreak Messenger guy to do it. He didn't even have the nerve to face her."

I stretched my ears back as far as they would go.

"That poor girl," Jennifer said. "To get dumped and not even have the chance to talk about it, to work things out."

Carmen didn't strike me as the talking type.

"Or to have a chance to knock the guy upside the head."

Now *that* was more Carmen's style.

"I wonder what he's like?"

"Who? Carmen's boyfriend?"

"No, the Heartbreak Messenger. He sounds so mysterious."

"He's probably tall and gorgeous. That way he can comfort you when he breaks the news."

I sat up just a little straighter in my seat.

"Are you kidding? He's probably short and dorky looking. That way, when he breaks up with the girl, she thinks, 'Well, could be worse. I could be dating *him*.'"

I slumped back down.

The girls giggled. Mr. Hogan looked our way, then turned and kept rambling on about some lady named Helen.

"Pssst." A girl on the other side of me, whose name I could never remember, waved her hand at the girls behind me. "I heard that the Heartbreak Messenger is actually a junior high kid."

I heard sputters of disbelief from the other

girls. "Not a chance," said Vicki. "If he was in junior high, no one would take him seriously."

I heard different versions of that conversation several times in the hallways and the lunchroom. For a while, it was a hot topic. Nobody really cared who the Heartbreak Messenger was—the mystery was the fun part. But just about everyone had an opinion about what he did. Most of the guys seemed okay with it, and most of the girls had issues. I just had fun listening and only worried a little that someone might figure out who *he* really was.

I had sworn Rob to secrecy, which I knew was a gamble. There were enough negative opinions about the Heartbreak Messenger's business that I didn't want to start getting hate mail in my locker. Or another fist in the eye. More important, if word ever got out about the rates I charged, people would start hitting me up to borrow money.

Apparently I wasn't the only one who wanted to remain anonymous. One afternoon I was watching an old classic movie in our apartment when the phone rang.

"Hello?" I answered with half a bologna sandwich in my mouth.

Silence greeted me on the other end, but I could tell someone was there. "Rob," I said, "if you ask me if my refrigerator's running again, I swear I'll . . ."

"Is this the Heartbreak Messenger?" a guy's voice interrupted.

I immediately put *Star Wars* on pause and cleared my throat. I hadn't had a phone client before—Mom said we couldn't afford a cell phone for me, and I didn't really want Marcus giving out our home number. But I could work with it.

"Sure is."

"Can you speak openly?"

I glanced around the empty apartment. "Uh, I think so."

"Her name is Sarah."

"Who's name is Sarah?"

"Your target."

Target? I suddenly hoped the caller hadn't gotten me confused with some Mafia hit man across town. "Are you her boyfriend?" I asked.

Silence. "Possibly."

I rolled my eyes. "Well, what's her boyfriend's name?"

"Why do you need to know?"

I strummed my fingers on the faded arms of the couch. "Maybe . . . so I can tell her who the message is from?"

The paranoid voice seemed to consider. "Her boyfriend's name is Doug."

"Okay. Where can I find Sa . . . uh, the target?"

"She spends her afternoons at the FFA farm out on Bluejacket Road."

Now we were getting somewhere. "All right. A lot of my customers . . ."

"I'll take the flowers, but she can buy her own chocolates. The money is under the doormat outside your front door. I need it done today." Then he hung up.

I tossed the phone on the couch and went out to look under the welcome mat. Sure enough, a wad of cash was stashed there in a plastic sandwich bag. Exact change.

I thought briefly about giving Marcus a raise. *Nah.*

Instead I went into my bedroom and pulled the flowers out of their cloudy water. I started yanking off all of the brown and shriveled parts, but that took too long because carnations have a lot of petals. I finally just grabbed a pair of scissors and hacked off any chunk of flower that seemed old. They didn't exactly look as good as new when I finished, but I was okay with that.

I paused at the kitchen counter to write Mom a note. She always had me do that, even though nine times out of ten I got back to the apartment before she did. Beside the notepad was a stack of unopened mail. I quickly glanced through it and stopped at an envelope with the bold, red words "Past Due" stamped right on the front.

I ripped the envelope open and scanned through the contents. It was the electric bill. *Last month's* electric bill for thirty-eight bucks. And it was weeks overdue.

I felt a black hole growing in my stomach. How could Mom not mention this to me? First the apartment, now the electricity. I couldn't decide which would be worse: not having a working TV, or not having an apartment to put it in.

Things had to be pretty bad if she couldn't pay a thirty-eight-dollar bill. I knew what I had to do.

I charged back to my room and pulled that amount from the stash in my sock drawer. I crammed the money and the bill into the pristine white envelope with the little cellophane window. I slapped a stamp onto it on my way down the apartment stairs and then dropped it into the mailbox. And I hoped our lights would still work when I came home.

Chapter 13

Within twenty minutes of the mysterious phone call, I was on my bike heading toward Bluejacket Road. Most kids on the west side of town cruised down that road at least three or four times a month during the summer. Bluejacket led to the widest and deepest part of the river, where rope swings hung from the sycamores like tinsel at Christmas. More broken arms and busted lips probably happened at that stretch of river than on any other body of water in the state.

I passed Root's Nursery and Farmer's Market not long after leaving town. Apples and walnuts spilled out of barrels in front of the store. A short while later I could see the two farms up ahead on the right. The first was a small dairy farm. Every kid in town visited that farm in the third grade, which made it seem friendly and wholesome. But the smell along that stretch of road was wicked enough to bring down a grown rhinoceros.

As I got closer, I began to take deep breaths, until just at the right moment I sucked in a lungful of air and pedaled triple-time for the next intersection. I was quick on my bike but even so, I had to start letting the air hiss out on the final stretch so my lungs didn't explode. I've never actually seen anyone pass out while riding through there, but some kids with smaller lungs swear that their hair comes out curlier on the other side.

I took the next turnoff and passed a white sign with blue letters: HOME OF THE FUTURE FARMERS OF AMERICA (FFA).

I had no idea where I was headed, but the dirt road leading to the small farm was smooth and well worn. It was set off from the dairy farm, but the smell of cow poop was quickly settling on the back of my tongue. I pulled my shirt collar up over my nose and mouth.

I headed toward the biggest building. It seemed to have the strongest smell, although the whole place was rich with animal fumes. I parked out front and poked my head around one of the tall wooden doors.

Cows. Lots of them. Each with their own stall. A guy with a pitchfork shoveled hay toward each cow, one by one. *Huh,* I thought. *People really do that.*

The guy, complete with cowboy boots and a plaid shirt, turned when the door creaked open. "Yeah?" he asked.

"Hi. Uh, howdy. I'm looking for Sarah."

"Goat kennels. That way." He gestured out the door to my right.

"Much obliged." I nodded and pinched the brim of my imaginary hat. When in Rome, you know . . .

I veered to the right, and then followed my nose from really disgusting to somewhat disgusting, arriving at a smaller building. The roof was low and made from plywood and wavy aluminum, and the door was hinged with super-strength twisty-ties. I gently pulled it open and stepped inside.

The long room was filled with metal pens painted bright green. Several goats milled around in each pen, eating, or sleeping, or just standing there. What a life. A girl with a long blond braid down her back sat on a three-legged stool next to one of the pens. She wore tight jeans and high leather work boots, and her plaid shirt was tied in a knot just above her belly button. She was stroking the head of an ugly brown goat, but she paused and looked up as I came in.

"Hi." She studied me for a minute, her eyebrows scrunched. "Are you one of the field trip kids from the elementary school?"

Ouch. I forced a laugh. "That's a good one." I tried to make my voice sound as deep as possible without slipping into my Darth Vader impression.

She forced a laugh, too.

"I'm looking for Sarah."

She studied me a little more, glanced down at the flowers in my hand, and then turned back to pat the goat's head. "I'm Sarah."

I looked around the building, trying hard to remember some of the one-liners I'd pulled off the Internet awhile ago. But all that came to mind was old Ben Kenobi, saying, "The Force will be with you always."

"Nice goats," I said instead.

"Yeah. Thirty-two of them. Ten males. And yet somehow they all get along." Sarah laughed nervously. Her eyes kept darting at me and then looking away, and her fingers fidgeted with the goat's ear.

"Um . . ." I said.

She interrupted before I could go on. Her voice was quiet, already defeated. She looked for all the world like she was talking to the goat, but she couldn't have been because she said, "I've heard you're just some junior high kid. Makes sense, really. Wouldn't work if you were a high-schooler. Somehow I thought you might be a little taller, though." She looked at me, eyes watery. "You are him, aren't you?" Her shaky voice dropped to a whisper. "The Heartbreak Messenger."

It was a statement, not a question.

And it struck me all at once, a single explosive idea. An idea so crazy that it never could have occurred to me without staring it in the face.

This high-schooler, this goat girl—older, taller, smarter, more experienced—she was afraid. Of *me*.

Afraid of this kid delivering a message. Afraid of what my visit would mean to her social life and her love life and whatever other lives high-schoolers have. From the second she recognized who I was, right up to the point where I finished delivering the message, she was terrified of me. The messenger.

A feeling of power suddenly surged through me, like taking a smooth jump on a bike. I felt ten feet tall, taller than Carmen Mendoza or any other senior whose fist I may come up against. Me. Bearer of messages that made every last high-schooler tremble with fear. Even the ones that wore Wranglers and hung out with goats.

I nodded graciously and held out the flowers. "I'm sorry to be the one to tell you. But your boyfriend did send me with a message."

She took the flowers and sniffed them, a sniff that turned into a sniffle as her eyes became even more watery. "We've only been together twenty-two-and-a-half days. I thought things were going so well, but you never know, do you? You never know what he's thinking, I mean. I guess he wasn't thinking about me."

Then the floodgates opened.

She cried and blubbered and then cried some more. Tears flowed like the fountain in front of city hall. I started to worry about her dehydrating. There wasn't anyone else there in the barn, and it didn't seem right to leave her alone like that, so I stood and watched her. I wasn't sure what else to do. I felt like I should put my arm around her and comfort her or something, but I didn't know how to do that or even if it would be appropriate, professionally speaking. So I just watched her cry.

Man, she was good at it.

It took her awhile, but she finally settled down, or at least went from choking sobs to pitiful sniffles. I didn't say a word, wishing for the hundredth time that I had a personal scriptwriter to hand me cool lines when I needed them. Finally I just reached over and patted her arm, which I hoped didn't violate any kind of workplace code of conduct or anything. "It's okay," I said, which probably sounded pretty dumb.

She eventually started plucking off the flower heads and feeding them to the goats. I was glad to see that because then I didn't feel nearly as guilty for giving her recycled funeral flowers.

It was about then that another girl walked in on the scene. She also wore jeans and boots, but her dark hair was cropped short around her ears. She wore a T-shirt that said "Manure happens." Her eyes grew wide when she saw us.

"Sarah! What's the matter?" She rushed over to my target's side and put her arm around her. The new girl looked up at me like I was shoving bamboo shoots under Sarah's fingernails.

Sarah sniffed. "It's the Heartbreak Messenger. Rick sent him to break up with me."

The new girl pulled Sarah closer and squeezed her tight. "That son of a . . ."

Rick? Sarah's last statement left a ringing in my ears.

I cleared my throat. "Um . . . ?"

The new girl shot me a death ray with her eyes. "You can leave, squirt."

"Yeah, okay." I pointed at Sarah. "But isn't your boyfriend's name . . . ex-boyfriend . . . isn't his name Doug?"

The new girl looked up at me sharply. "My boyfriend's name is Doug."

I pointed at Sarah again. "But your name is Sarah." There may have been a touch of panic in my voice.

The new girl stood up, towering over me. "She's Sarah with an *H*. I'm Sara with an *A*. My boyfriend's name is Doug."

Oh, boy. I scratched my head, cleared my throat again, and then took what was left of the flowers out of Sarah's (note the *H*) limp hand. I pushed them toward Sara (no *H*).

"In that case, these are for you."

Sara crossed her arms and stared at me. More death rays. But now she was shooting them out at me from behind a trickle of tears. I laid the flowers down at her feet. Time to go.

I turned to Sarah. "Really very sorry. I mean it. Really. But, hey, good news for you, right?"

She looked confused, which was understandable. But at least she'd stopped crying.

I didn't dare look back at Sara as I turned and hightailed it to my bike.

Personally, I think the chocolates would have made a big difference.

Chapter 14

- - - ➤

➤

Abby became a lot busier after our conversation in the gutter. Apparently dating a blunder-brain keeps you pretty swamped. She did manage to spend time with Rob and me every once in a while, mostly because our after-school homework sessions were still her best bet for scoring decent grades in the classes we shared. It definitely wasn't the same, though. Our studying became all business. No more goofing off or fooling around or seeing if we could make Abby laugh and snort her orange juice. Just grammar and geometry and Jack London.

When I showed up late at Mick's one day, I was glad to see Abby there. She and Rob already had their notebooks out and were deep in conversation. But as I approached, Rob gave me a sheepish grin, opened his backpack wide, and pulled it over his head. Abby squinted at me and folded her arms.

"What's up, guys?" I looked from one to the other. "Why's Rob playing ostrich?"

Abby just stared at me.

I looked down at my watch. "I'm not even that late."

"I have three questions for you," she finally said.

This can't be good.

"Do you remember my cousin Audrey?" she asked, holding up one finger.

"Um, yeah, I think so."

"Her best friend Sara was dumped earlier this week by her boyfriend."

I felt my face getting hot. I couldn't let my ears turn red. *Cool thoughts. Sherbet. Icicles. Snowball in the face.*

"Only he didn't do the dumping," she continued. "He used that Heartbreak Messenger guy." She raised a second finger. "Have you heard of him?"

I found myself staring at Abby's hand instead of her face. Only one more finger to go. *Time to stall*.

"Have I heard of your cousin's best friend's ex-boyfriend?"

Abby didn't say anything. She just narrowed her eyes into razor-thin slits. *So much for stalling*.

"I've heard the rumors." I tried to keep my voice as level as possible.

"Well, I mentioned that incident to Rob just now." Abby lifted a third finger. "Do you have any idea what he said?"

Oh, here we go. "I can only imagine," I said, staring at the ostrich.

"It just slipped out, Quentin," said Rob, emerging from his backpack. "I couldn't help it."

Abby's outstretched arm fell to her side, her fingers closing into a fist. "You really are the Heartbreak Messenger? The punky kid who charges people to break up with their girlfriends?"

"That's four questions . . . no, five."

"I can't believe it, Quentin!"

"It's not a big deal."

"Not a big deal? You're wrecking people's lives for money!"

"Come on, Abby," Rob chimed in. "It's not like he's breaking the law."

Abby turned to stare at Rob. He placed a hand on his backpack, ready to climb back inside.

With a hard laugh, she said, "No, he's not breaking the law. He's just breaking hearts—" She turned back to me. "And watching girls cry. I can't believe it. Why would you do that?"

I felt the blood drain from my face and start pounding through my veins. "Because it's good business. Plus I'm providing a community service."

"Since when does helping guys act like cowards count as a community service?"

"Hey, don't blame me. It would still happen in the end, you know, even if I didn't do it. They'd still break up."

Abby rolled her eyes. "But how do you think Sara felt knowing her own boyfriend didn't care enough about her to break up with her face-to-face?"

"I don't know. We didn't talk much about feelings."

"That's right." Abby pointed a finger at me. Just one. "Nobody's thinking about the girl's feelings here. You aren't, and the guy that's paying you money sure isn't. It's wrong, Quentin."

"Breaking up is hard to do." An image of Carmen just before she'd hit me sprang to mind and I knew I was speaking the absolute truth. "Who wouldn't want to get out of it?"

Rob raised his hand. "I think Quentin has a good point there." He gave me a quick nod and a thumbs-up. I wouldn't be forgiving him any time soon, but he probably figured jumping on my bandwagon counted for something.

"That's just it," Abby said. "Some things are hard for a reason."

"Give it a rest," I said. "Whether they hire me or not, they're still going to break up. I just help them get things done sooner so that everyone can move on with their lives."

Abby folded her arms. "If Justin ever broke up with me—which isn't going to happen, by the way—I'd want him to sit down with me in person, like a man."

A huge grin spread across Rob's face. He swung his legs over the table and sat in front of me. He took my hand and lowered his voice an octave.

"Abigail, my love, our relationship stinks like yesterday's garbage, you're way too intelligent for my tastes, and another artist has come into my life."

I smiled and raised my voice to a falsetto. "Oh, that's okay, Justin. I just want you to know how much I appreciate you telling me that yourself."

Rob and I broke out laughing.

Abby stared at us, lips tight. Then she grabbed her notebook from the table and shoved it into her backpack. She zipped it up, got up from the table, and stopped in front of me. "You've sold your soul for a couple of bucks, Quentin. I always thought you were better than that." She spun around and stalked off.

Suddenly, I didn't feel like laughing. I watched her go, her golden blond hair bouncing with each step, until she turned up the street and out of sight.

The blood that had been pulsing red in my veins quickly cooled, leaving behind a numb desire to go back and try that conversation again.

"You know, Quentin," Rob said, "she's right. If you really have sold your soul for a couple of bucks, you should go back and renegotiate. You're getting ripped off."

Chapter 15

There was no doubt about it, Abby had changed, and not for the better. I hadn't noticed it right away, but looking back I realized she had been acting weird for several weeks. And the way she took the news about me being the Heartbreak Messenger clinched it. The old Abby wouldn't have gotten upset about it. She would have rolled her eyes and called me a dweeb or something. The new Abby was a whole different story. She'd apparently crossed over to the dark side.

And from what I could tell, that was all Justin Masterturd's fault. Not only was he a complete moron, but now he was costing me a best friend. He was really starting to annoy me.

Once Abby found out about my business venture, she practically gave Rob and I the silent treatment. I quickly realized how much harder my math and science homework were without her around. And I had plenty of time to struggle through it on my own, because it had been almost two weeks since my last messenger job. The first of the month was approaching and Mom was probably starting to freak out about where the rent money would come from.

I still heard Heartbreak Messenger talk here and there, and Marcus assured me he was working up a few more customers, but I started to wonder if that was the end of it. There were other business strategies I hadn't tried yet—approaching potential customers in the high school locker rooms, handing out fliers at football games, setting up a Web site. But for the most part my secret identity was still intact, and I wanted to hold on to that for as long as I could.

I was seriously considering putting up a few anonymous posters—just a reminder that the

Heartbreak Messenger was out there—when my next client found me.

Rob and I were on our bikes heading for Lincoln Hill Park, a grassy area hidden above the neighborhoods on the west side of town. We had an assignment for our physical science class to watch the night skies. We were almost there when Rob shouted from behind me, "By the way . . . Marcus asked me to tell you something."

"What?" I yelled over my shoulder.

"He said that he sent someone your way."

I squeezed the brakes and Rob zipped past me. We were entering the parking lot next to the park, so I slid off my bike as Rob waited for me to catch up with him. "Is that all he said?" I asked.

"Yep. What is that, some sort of Messenger code or something?"

"If it is, then he forgot to give me the code book. I mean, he didn't say who, or where to meet them, or anything?"

"Nope. He did say you should get a cell phone."

"That's helpful."

"Hey, don't look at me. I'm just the messenger here. Speaking of that . . ." He gave me a sidelong glance. "You know, if you ever needed help with the Messenger thing, I'd be happy to pitch in. I've been trying to find ways to make money, but I haven't had much luck so far. When I told my mom, she gave me a bucket of walnuts she bought at the farmers' market and said she'd give me five bucks if I cracked them all. Five bucks! Can you believe it? It'll take me weeks to get through that bucket."

We pushed our bikes toward the paved trail that headed up the hill to the park. There were a dozen other kids hanging around the trail ahead of us. An older man glared at them as he came down the trail with his dog on a leash. A group of high school football players trotted past us up the hill, their counting chant of "One-two-three-four" keeping time with their heavy footfalls. Just before we came to the trailhead, I noticed a guy leaning on a motorcycle beneath a lamppost at the far end of the parking lot.

He wore a long black leather jacket over a white T-shirt, and—even though it was already getting dark—he sported a pair of expensive sunglasses. But despite the shades, I could tell he was staring right at me. As I looked his way, he nodded in my direction. A tiny movement that made my palms sweat.

"Hey, Quentin, let's go. Most of the good spots are probably taken already."

I barely heard Rob. This guy in the leather jacket was smooth. The way he stood, the way he moved, the way he held his head so that his hair just barely fell in front of his eyes. He was like the lone gunslinger without a past that strides into town and who everybody stares at and thinks, *He's smooth*. But I knew this guy was different. He did have a past—one he wanted to be done with.

My money-making senses were tingling: He was looking for me.

"Hey, Rob," I said. "Did Marcus know we were coming here tonight?"

"Yeah. I asked him yesterday if he could give me a ride. He said he'd give me a ride if I gave him my room."

"Why don't you go on without me?"

"What? Why?"

"It's nothing. I'll be there in a few minutes."

He followed my gaze to the cool character

beneath the lamppost. "Sweet bike. I've seen that motorcycle parked in the high school lot. Who is that?"

"The guy I need to talk to. I think."

"Oh. That. Messenger stuff. Hey, let me come with you."

"What? Why?"

Rob shrugged. "I dunno. I'm curious. What do you say, and what do they say and all that."

"Rob, this is official business."

"He's waiting for a seventh-grader in an empty parking lot. How official could it be?"

"My clients want their privacy. It's part of why they come to me."

"Please? Just this once?"

I couldn't exactly tell him this kind of work required the ability to keep your mouth shut. "Not a chance, Rob. I'll catch you in a few minutes."

Rob grabbed my arm and dropped his voice. "Hey, how do you know he's a customer? How do you know he's not just waiting for everyone to clear so he can jump you?"

"All my money is at home in my sock drawer, so he's going to be disappointed."

"Well, maybe he's some girl's older brother, here to beat you to a bloody pulp for a message you delivered."

"Come on, Rob, just let me go."

"Fine." He scowled at me and gripped his handlebars hard. "But if I hear you screaming like a little girl in a few minutes, I'm not going to come running back to save your butt. Just so you know."

He pushed off with his bike and headed up the trail.

I turned and headed for another twenty-five bucks.

At least, I thought I was. Rob's comment about the guy being some girl's older brother had shaken me just a bit. I mean, would Marcus really have told someone that they could find me marching up the trail to Lincoln Hill Park? I took a few deep breaths.

The guy didn't move as I approached, except to turn his head for a second to spit. He was tall with wide shoulders—probably a high school senior. I stopped at what I figured was a safe distance in front of him and lowered the kickstand on my bike. I glanced behind me, hoping to find a few stragglers still passing through the parking lot. But the last person in sight was just cresting the top of the hill.

I swallowed back the nervous lump in my throat. "You looking for me?" I asked the stranger.

He smiled a tight, wicked smile. "You got quite a gig going on here, Sly."

"What do you mean?"

"I hear you're the little genius that's charging people to break up with their girlfriends."

"I deliver messages. That's all."

He held up his hands. "I'm cool with that, man. I'm all about good communication. But I'm a little curious, Sly. What do you do with all those tears?"

"Tears?"

"Yeah. Don't the ladies cry when you 'communicate' with them?"

I folded my arms, thinking about Goat Girl and the cry-fest she'd had. "Yeah. Sometimes. My messages aren't exactly happy ones."

He shook his head. "Man, you must have a heart of stone."

That made me blink. A heart of stone? I was just the messenger.

The guy sighed. "Not me, man. Not me. I have

an eye for the ladies and they have an eye for me." He removed his sunglasses and gestured toward himself. "But really, can you blame them?"

This guy's nuts, I thought. *But at least he's not going to mug me.* "So is there anything I can do for you? It's getting late."

The wicked smile leaped back to his face. "Now that you mention it, I could use your help. In fact, I should tell you up front that I could become one of your best customers. You might say I kind of have relationship ADHD."

I had no idea what he meant, but I knew I could use a "best customer."

"At the moment I'm interested in, well, doing some house cleaning. Simplifying. Downsizing. Starting over, you could say."

"What's her name?" I asked, reaching for my pocket. By now I carried a pen and notecards with me just about everywhere I went.

"Janine."

"OK. Where can I find her?"

Motorcycle Guy placed his sunglasses slowly back on his face.

"Well, now, she's just the first one."

I stopped trying to figure out how to spell Janine and looked up. "First one?"

Even behind his sunglasses he looked like a kid that just got caught with both hands in the cookie jar. "Told you . . . relationship ADHD. It's so hard to stay focused sometimes."

"So . . . are you telling me you have more than one girlfriend you need to break up with?"

"Elizabeth . . . she goes by Lizzy."

I scribbled down the name. "Okay. And where can I find these two?"

"And Bethany. Oh . . . can't forget Bethany. But I'm gonna try real hard."

"Three girlfriends? At the same time?" Where did this guy think he was, the African pride lands?

"You got it, Sly. Now go free me up so I can rest awhile before setting my eyes on the next conquest."

"I assume the girls don't know about each other."

The guy shifted his weight off the motorcycle and leaned toward me. I resisted the urge to step back. "No they don't. And you're not going to tell 'em. Right?"

"'Course not."

"Swear to it, Sly."

"I swear I won't tell them."

Motorcycle Guy stared at me from behind his glasses. "I don't believe you," he finally said. "Swear on the Beast."

"On the what?"

He stepped aside and gestured toward his motorcycle. "Do it."

Since laughing out loud didn't seem advisable, I stepped forward and put my hand on the worn black leather seat of his Kawasaki. "I swear I won't tell them about one another."

His shoulders relaxed a little. Reaching inside his leather jacket, he pulled out a small black book. He thumbed through it, found a page near the middle, and held it out in front of me. "Addresses. All three of them."

I scribbled them down. When I'd finished, I carefully folded the paper as I thought about how to approach what came next.

"Now, since I'm going to deliver three messages, I'll need to charge you for all three. But I can give you a good discount."

"Not so fast, Sly. I was told it'd cost me twenty-five bucks to get this done. And that's what you'll get."

"You're asking me to track down three different girls." I spread my hands out. "That's three times as much work. . . ."

As I spoke, the guy reached back into his jacket pocket. With a sudden flick, a knife was in his hand. The streetlamp above us clicked on, as if waiting for its cue. Light glinted off the exposed blade.

My heart leaped into my throat. I immediately promised to take Rob's warnings more seriously. I didn't even have to swear on the Beast for that one.

He studied the blade for a moment, as though considering its craftsmanship in the halo of yellow light. His face looked all the more threatening with the new shadows. Then he lowered the knife and started cleaning his fingernails with the tip.

"Twenty-five should do it, don't you think, Sly?"

My teeth were clenched tight with fear or

anger, or both. "I don't suppose I can interest you in flowers or chocolates?"

He folded the blade and slipped it into his pocket in one smooth motion. Then he swung his leg over the motorcycle. "Nope. Just get the job done, Sly. Be sure to tell the ladies that Gunner sent you." With a downward kick, his motorcycle roared to life. He pulled a wad of bills out of his pocket and tossed them at my feet. "See you 'round, Heartbreaker." And with a second roar, he sped off into the dusk.

Right there I decided it was okay to dislike some clients.

As I picked up the money, I noticed something lying on the pavement a few feet away. Small and rectangular, his black book blended into the asphalt, like a secret desperately wanting to stay hidden. Looking around at the empty street, I reached down and grabbed the book.

The pages were crisp but full. Names—all girls—numbers, addresses, dates, and notes covered the pages. A detailed history of short-term relationships and other secret tidbits that Gunner obviously thought should stay hidden. A gold mine of information that I silently slipped into my pocket with the money. I smiled to myself.

My mind was spinning with ideas. I didn't know what I was going to do with Gunner's three girlfriends, but I was sure of one thing. No one pulls a knife on the Heartbreak Messenger, short-changes him, and rides off on a motorcycle. No one.

Chapter 16

➤

Shortly after the echo of Gunner's Kawasaki faded into the deepening night, I was tripping over seventh-graders at the top of Lincoln Hill. "Rob!" I called out over the chitchat of a dozen conversations.

"Yo, Quentin!" I heard him shout from across the field. I found him lying on his back next to Abby, which surprised me.

"Hey, Abby."

"Hey," she said, keeping her eyes fixed on the domed sky above us.

"Nice of you to stop by. I would have thought you'd bring Justin along." I didn't use any of my usual nicknames for Bulky Sweater Man, since I'd decided to try extra hard to get on Abby's good side again.

Abby studied the ends of her hair, although she probably couldn't see much in the dark. "He said he'd meet me here. I'm sure he's on his way."

I lay down on my back next to them, our heads close together, our legs stretching out like spokes in a bike wheel. A gentle breeze passed through the dark night air, which felt cool on my face.

"Seen anything yet?" I asked.

"Nothing but stars so far," Abby said.

"What are we looking for again?" Rob asked.

"The Orionids," I said.

"Is that a rock band or a stomach virus?" he shot back.

"Meteors, you dope. Just keep your eyes open and count the shooting stars," I said.

Rob wasn't in our physical science class, so technically he didn't need to be there. But Abby and I, along with three of Mr. Baumbaker's periods, were supposed to be counting meteors. Our teacher had recommended Lincoln Hill Park since it sat secluded on the west side of town. The backside of the hill sloped away from the lights of the town, into a wooded area that eventually met up with Bluejacket Road. The hilltop was ringed by sycamores, but opened up in the middle of the park to provide a wide view of the sky.

"Oh, I just saw a whole bunch," Rob said.

"Poking yourself in the eye doesn't count," Abby said. "Only real shooting stars."

The grass was soft and kind of tickled my ears. There was something mesmerizing about staring at the sky. After a while it seemed like you could feel the whole Earth spinning underneath you.

"How will I know when I see one?" Rob asked.

"It will be the only one of those bright dots up there that's shooting across the sky," I said.

"I wonder where he is?" Abby said.

"Who," Rob asked, "the Orionid?"

"Justin. He should have been here by now."

"Oh, I just saw one!" I said, my arm shooting upward. That statement may or may not have been true.

"Where?" Abby said. "How's this going to work? I can't watch the whole sky at the same time."

We lay there in silence for a while, feeling

overwhelmed as the stars seemed to multiply and grow brighter, and the slivered moon watched us from the horizon.

"Hey, Rob," I finally said. "I think I see Cassiopeia. It's that *W* right there. Do you remember who she was? Someone from mythology or something?" Our Cub Scout days had been brief, with lots of throwing rocks into large bodies of water, but not much astronomy.

Rob didn't answer.

"Rob?"

Abby laughed. "He's asleep."

Rob confirmed that with a soft snore.

"Rob McFallen, the learned astronomer," I said.

"Well, so far he's not missing much."

I scanned the sky, working hard to keep my own eyes open. My mind wandered as I thought about Gunner on his motorcycle, the little black book in my pocket, and my ex–best friend beside me. And then suddenly I saw one. A star streaked across the sky for just an instant, like a shimmering fish through black waters, and then disappeared. But its brilliant shadow glowed in my eyes for a moment longer.

"I saw it!" Abby shrieked. "I've never seen one before."

"There's another!"

"Three!"

"Four. Five!"

An excited murmur ran through the other groups of kids sprawled on the grass. We waited a moment. Not breathing. Hoping for more.

And they came.

We didn't try to count. Maybe five or six at a time touched the blackness and disappeared. Then another wave, then another. Skipping, streaking, skating on the sky. We didn't take a breath for a while, even after everything came to a rest and all the stars froze in place once again.

We must have shifted our bodies to get a better view of the meteors, because when I finally took a breath, I realized the side of Abby's upside-down face was touching mine. She didn't pull away and neither did I. There was something about what we had just seen in the sky, something extraordinary and unreal, something that could never be explained, only shared. And somehow, knowing that

I had shared it with Abby right there next to me, made it all the more meaningful.

"Wow," Abby whispered.

"You don't see that every day."

"Wow," she whispered again.

We lay there for a while in silence, her cheek warm against mine. The feeling of what we had just seen was fading quickly, and I tried hard to hold on to it.

"I wonder where they go?" she finally said.

"Probably burn up in the atmosphere or something."

"How sad. It's not until the very end that they turn into something beautiful, and then they die. Kind of like a flower."

"Yeah, but what a way to go."

We watched for more meteors, but I half-hoped that no more would come. Anything else would have been anticlimactic.

"There's so many stars out here," said Abby. "I think I see Orion."

"Where?"

"Right there. See those three stars? I think that's his belt."

"Cool." I didn't tell her that Orion wouldn't be in the sky until early in the morning.

"Where was that one you were talking about before?"

"Cassiopeia. Right there. It's shaped like a W. I think she was a queen. A queen that was full of herself, if I remember right."

"What about that star there? I think that one's a planet, right? It's red, so it must be Mercury."

"No. Probably Mars," I said. "Red planet, named for the god of war."

"I thought Mercury was the god of war."

"No, it was Mars. I don't remember who Mercury was . . . wait, he was the messenger for Jupiter." As soon as I said it, I knew it was a mistake.

"Oh?" she said. "Did he go around breaking hearts, too?"

And suddenly the moment, the good-ol'-days moment, was over. "Let's not go there," I said.

"Sorry. I didn't mean to discuss anything that might remind you that you have a conscience."

"Hey, are you ready for the English quiz tomorrow?" I asked.

"You're just trying to change the subject."

"Yes, but we do have a quiz tomorrow."

"Nuh-uh."

"Yuh-huh."

Abby jumped up. "I saw Alyssa over there earlier. I'm going to ask her." She started forward but hit her foot on Rob's leg. "Sorry, Rob," she said as she headed off toward another group of kids.

"What's up?" Rob said as he sat up with his eyes half-open.

"Nothing much. Just discussing some mythology. Hey, I noticed Justin Mastersnob didn't make it tonight."

"Yeah, that's a shame." Rob grinned, wide awake. "I hope he didn't have bike trouble."

"You want to tell me how you did it?"

Rob laid back down and put his hands behind his head. "I don't know what you're talking about. But I wouldn't be surprised if Justin's bike chain shows up in his mail box tomorrow."

I snorted. "Classic." I could almost forgive Rob for spilling the beans to Abby.

Almost.

Chapter 17

Two days later I also had sabotage on my mind. Not bike sabotage—at least not *bicycle* sabotage. Something different. Something that had taken a bit of quick but careful planning.

"And what is the purpose of your reservation?" The librarian looked down at me over the top of her reading glasses. The public library had been closed the day before, so this part of my plan was a little behind schedule.

I scratched my head for a moment. "A group discussion on the social habits of the male African lion." It was close enough to the truth.

The librarian scribbled the information into

her reservation book. "How very interesting. A biology class?"

"Um, more like sociology."

"I see. Study Room One is all yours at four o'clock. Please be sure to read the rules and leave the place spick-and-span."

"Um," I hesitated, not sure how far to push my luck. "Can I get Study Room Two?"

She pursed her lips. "The rooms are exactly the same."

"Well . . . I like to use even numbers whenever I can. Superstition." I smiled, as though I stood up for even numbers all the time.

"Uh-huh." She studied me for a moment and then scribbled a little more in her book. "All right, then. Study Room Two. Just remember—two is an even number, but it's also a prime. And primes are not to be trusted."

"Right . . . thanks." Now it was my turn to wonder if she was serious or not. Instead, I headed toward Study Room Two with a glance at the clock. Five minutes until four. I made a few quick preparations, read the rules posted on the wall, and then ducked into the nearby gardening section. I picked a horticulture book from the shelf and opened it, holding it up close to my face. I didn't really look at the pages, except for the one that showed a picture of a mutant tomato the size of a man's head. Crazy. My eyes peeked over the top of the book, focused on the study room entrance.

As the clock struck four, the room was still empty. I tossed the horticulture book onto a nearby shelf and pulled off another. Plant breeding. No color pictures.

My plan was a good one and I was determined to make it work. The encounter with Gunner had left me steaming.

I didn't like threats. I hated a cheater.

I wondered if he would have treated me differently if I'd been a high-schooler. But that didn't matter. I wasn't just any kid. I was the Heartbreak Messenger. I inspired fear and demanded respect. Others might tremble at a tough dude with a knife, but I had powers that Motorcycle Guy didn't even realize existed.

Assuming anyone showed up.

At 4:01, a girl approached the room. She had thick-rimmed glasses and a ponytail dangling above plain clothes. Pretty, but she screamed "nerd." She stood in the doorway and looked around, like it might have been booby-trapped. On the whiteboard I'd written, "Please come in and sit down." She saw that, looked around one more time, and then took a seat. There were three envelopes in front of her on the table. She picked one up, looked at it briefly, and then put it down.

A minute later another high school girl approached and looked into the room. She was also pretty and walked with a bouncing grace, but her clothes were more artsy than trendy. If she had been a junior high student, I would have said "drama club."

She pulled a 3x5 card out of her pocket and gestured toward Pretty Nerd. "Hey. Can you tell me what this is about?"

The other girl held up a similar card. "I got one, too. I just arrived."

Drama Queen hesitated for a second. "This better be good," she grumbled as she took a seat.

The two didn't say a word to each other for three and a half minutes. Drama Queen drummed her fingers. Pretty Nerd pulled out a book and started reading, but looked up every five seconds. I could tell they were getting antsy, and I was afraid I'd have to settle for two and step in before they decided to leave.

But then number three arrived. Very pretty. Well dressed. Probably very popular. She didn't stop at the doorway and look around. She walked right in, held up a card, and said, "Who sent me this?" The other two girls held up their cards, too. The Popular One rolled her eyes and looked down at her own card.

She read, "'I have information that will profoundly affect the rest of your life. It has to do with your boyfriend.' Is that what yours says, too?"

The other girls nodded.

The Popular One rolled her eyes again. "All right. I'm gone."

Then I stepped into the room. I was all business, swinging the door closed behind me without even looking. "Sit down," I said to the Popular One as I strode up to the whiteboard like I was a teacher.

She sat, probably more out of surprise than anything.

I uncapped a red dry-erase marker and wrote in big bold letters, "I am the Heartbreak Messenger."

Then I replaced the marker, put my hands flat down on the table, and looked at them. They stared at me.

I knew I had to be very careful. I had sworn that I wouldn't tell Gunner's girlfriends about one another. I was going to keep that promise, and I was going to break up with his girlfriends for him. And that was all I'd do for him.

But to accomplish all that, and hopefully a little extra, I pretty much couldn't say a word. Who knows what motorcycle nightmares I might have if I broke an oath on the Beast?

Drama Queen finally spoke first. "Okay, so what now? You break up with people's girlfriends for them, right? So why are we here?"

I stared at them, calm as the ocean. At least on the outside.

"So you're going to, what? Tell me that my boyfriend is breaking up with me? I don't think so," the Popular One said.

Come on, somebody say it, I pleaded silently.

Drama Queen tossed her card toward me. "You

can forget that. No junior high squirt is going to make me stay longer in a library than I need to."

Then Pretty Nerd spoke, quietly, but with confidence. "Did Gunner send you?"

The other two girls' heads snapped so fast in the direction of the Pretty Nerd that I was surprised there weren't any spinal cord injuries.

Bingo.

"How do you know about Gunner?" asked the Popular One.

Drama Queen slowly turned her head toward the Popular One. "How do *you* know about Gunner?"

The Popular One lifted her chin another inch. "He happens to be my boyfriend."

"*Your* boyfriend?" Drama Queen replied, halfway out of her seat.

"Yeah. We've kept it kind of a secret. His grandma's Jewish and if she found out he was going out with a gentile, she'd die of a heart attack."

Drama Queen stared at the Popular One for a good long second before looking away. "Funny," she said, deflated. "He told me to keep our relationship a secret because his dad was in prison and he didn't want to drag my name through the mud."

The Popular One's jaw dropped. "You've been dating Gunner? How long?"

Drama Queen shrugged. "Two months."

"Why that rotten . . ." The Popular One suddenly found herself speechless. I was glad, since "No Cussing" was on the list of study-room rules.

The two girls sat in stunned silence for a minute before turning to Pretty Nerd. "So why are you here?" the Popular One asked.

The Pretty Nerd rolled her eyes. "Gunner told me to keep *our* relationship secret because that would make it more exciting. I figured he was seeing someone else, but I didn't care. I liked having his attention." She snapped her book closed. "Of course, I didn't think he was seeing *two* other girls besides me."

Then the room fell silent again. I could feel the dust settling and the truth sinking in. The Popular One dropped her head into her hands. Drama Queen cracked her knuckles. Pretty Nerd straightened her glasses. Eventually they all looked up at me.

"So that's it?" Drama Queen said. "He's breaking up with us all at once? Dumping the whole lot and moving on to a new group of unsuspecting victims?"

The Popular One swore. So much for rule number seven.

I cleared my throat and looked meaningfully down at the table. Except for Pretty Nerd, no one had noticed the envelopes. One by one they now reached for the envelopes in front of them and tore it open.

The Popular One dumped out a little black book.

Drama Queen dumped out a cheap tire pressure gauge with the name "Mickelson's" on the side.

The Pretty Nerd pulled out another 3x5 card.

The Popular One thumbed through the book. "This is full of names and numbers." She flipped the pages, soaking it in. "Samantha, Bethany, Karyn, Lizzy . . ." She broke off and looked at Drama Queen. "You're Lizzy, aren't you?"

"And I'm Bethany," the Pretty Nerd added.

The Popular One stuck a finger on a page and

stared. "And I'm Janine." She flipped to the front of the book, and then grinned. "This is Gunner's book. All the girls he's gone out with. Maybe some he hasn't yet. There's even some notes in here."

Drama Queen slowly tapped the pressure gauge against the palm of her hand. "You know, I think you can use this little thing to let the air out of someone's tire. I've never tried it before, but I'm sure I could learn."

The Popular One was still flipping page-by-page through the little book. "I can think of a few ways to make that three-timer's life a little more difficult with this. . . ."

Pretty Nerd brought up the index card and read, "Revenge is a dish best served cold." She blinked. "That's a bit over the top. But I'm the Web administrator for the student e-mail listing. Let me know what you have in mind with that little black book, and I'm sure there's a way I can help out."

The Popular One smiled wickedly. "Well, for starters, I'm thinking we totally hit him where it hurts the most. First . . ."

I knew that if I stayed any longer, I might be considered an accomplice. With their attention squarely on the Popular One, I slipped along the wall and out the door. I glanced back through the window of Study Room Two to see the ex-girlfriends with their heads together. A feeling of wicked triumph welled up inside of me.

My job there was finished. Gunner was free.

And in a whole heap of trouble.

Chapter 18

"Now there's someone just looking for trouble."

At the sound of her voice I paused, mid-step, and turned to come face-to-face with Abby. The sidewalk on West Oak was littered with fall leaves, and I realized I must have been deep in thought for her to get so close without me noticing. "Nah. I'm just looking for a book of stamps."

"Stamps? Like for mailing a letter?" Abby said. She fell into pace with me as we walked, her backpack bouncing gently with each step. "Do people still use those?"

"I guess so. You know, those old-timers who

still think the Internet is just a fad. Mick asked me to run and get some. Where are you going?"

"Isabelle's house. A group project for Spanish."

We walked together for half a block without speaking. Abby and I had never really talked about her reaction to me being the Heartbreak Messenger. But it had loomed over us ever since, like the Goodyear blimp. Part of me kind of wished she would bring it up so I could have a second chance to defend my chosen profession. But the rest of me would have been happy to see her let go of the whole thing altogether, or at least pretend it didn't bother her.

I glanced at her, studied the clouds, managed to find a fire hydrant fascinating, and then finally said, "So. How you doing, stranger?"

"Stranger? I see you in class every day."

"Yeah, but . . . you know." I crunched through a pile of leaves. Abby shuffled through them with several light kicks. I wanted to say that I missed having her around, that I missed the good old days, that—

"So how'd you do on that algebra test today?" she asked.

I glanced her way again and wondered if she was okay with being a stranger.

"Well," I said. "When lunchtime came I saw variables floating in my fruit cup."

Abby laughed. "Oh, come on. It couldn't have been that bad."

"What about you? Piece of cake, right?"

"Well . . ."

"Yeah. Don't hold back, now. What about your *Call of the Wild* essay? Did you finish?"

"More or less. I still have issues with that whole theme and symbols thing. I mean, the writer was just telling a story. He didn't decide on a theme and throw in a bunch of symbols that no one but an English teacher was going to notice."

"Well, we all see things differently, I guess."

Abby fiddled with the zipper on her jacket. *Zzziippp* down. *Zzziippp* up. "Hey, speaking of English. Um. I was wondering if I could come and study with you and Rob tomorrow."

I glanced over at her, but she was looking straight ahead.

"Yeah. Sure. I mean, we never kicked you out."

Zzziippp down. "Of course, I know that. It's

just, well, I haven't been doing too well in English lately and my mom says I need to shape up—and in history—or I can't do the photography class at the community center. And . . . other things."

I figured "other things" included going out with an eighth-grader. I briefly considered what might happen if I said no. But it was Abby.

"Sure. I mean, Rob hasn't been the same since you stopped hanging with us anyway."

Abby smiled. "Well, it's nice to be needed. I'm sure the real problem is that you guys need some hobbies. You know, go find a girlfriend or something."

I crunched through another pile of leaves. Harder this time. "Yeah, well, maybe someday."

"I don't understand why you don't like girls, Quentin."

I stopped walking. I looked at her. She looked back.

It seemed like a long time before a car passed by and broke our gaze. I blinked and turned my head. "Who said I didn't like girls? I just don't need a girlfriend. Not right now, at least."

Abby's eyes looked past me as she retreated

into her own thoughts. Then she suddenly glanced up at the building behind her. "Oh. Look. The post office. I probably ought to get going anyway."

"See you tomorrow?"

"Yeah. Tomorrow." *Zzziippp* up. And off she went.

I entered the post office but then immediately turned to look out the window as Abby crossed the street, her hands stuffed into her jacket pockets. Questions tumbled through my mind like a collection of bouncy balls in the clothes dryer. Did Abby really just happen to bump into me on West Oak? Or did she follow me there to talk with me? And if she did want to talk with me, was she really interested in still being friends, or did she just want help with her homework?

And why the heck am I feeling so confused?

I bought the stamps and kept the change (which was a lot less than Mick suggested it might be) and headed back. I'd walked about a block when I noticed a silver Mustang driving toward me. It was sweet. One of those with the low spoiler and chrome rims and black pinstriping on the sides. As it passed me, the wheels screeched in a tight U-turn and it pulled up beside me, heading the wrong way on the empty street.

I wasn't exactly sure what to do, so I went right on walking. The Mustang kept pace with me. I glanced over and saw an absolutely gorgeous high school blonde in the driver's seat with another girl next to her. I'd seen the other girl before—maybe a friend of Marcus or his former girlfriend. They were both staring at me.

"You the Heartbreak Messenger?" the blond girl asked.

Visions of hired assassins and ex-girlfriends with a vendetta sprang to my mind. I considered bolting, but even if I ran for my life at top speed, I'd never beat out a V8 with 315 horsepower. So I did the next best thing. I turned my head suavely and said, "Yeah." My voice only cracked a little.

The girl stopped the car and put it in park. I kept walking.

"I've got a job for you, if you're interested."

I hesitated for a moment before turning around. Somehow it had never occurred to me that I might have a female customer. I suppose that's just a little sexist, but hey, I'm a guy. As far as I knew, it was the guys who did the breaking up. Well, at least that's what I thought.

I approached the car, still worried that it might be some trick. Maybe she had Carmen and half of the girls' soccer team in the backseat, ready to spring out and jump me. They'd tie me up with carnation stems and shove chocolates down my throat while beating me over the head with the movie script of my life. Then I realized it would be hard to have anyone spring out of a two-door pony car, so I took a few more steps.

She looked me up and down, but didn't seem too impressed. Maybe she expected someone taller. "I'm Lisa," she said. "You got a pen?" She spoke to me like she was ordering a hamburger or something. But, wow, her eyes sparkled like polished headlights.

I handed her the pen from my pocket. She grabbed a scrap of paper from the console and scribbled something on it. Then she shoved the pen and paper into my hands. "That's the heart I want you to break. I want you to break it hard. I want to hear it crack all the way on the other side of town. Got it?"

The letters were kind of squished together.

"Duke Ripling," I read. The name seemed vaguely familiar. There was an address below the name. "Is this your boyfriend?"

She looked at me like I was a three-year-old with a snotty nose. "If he was my cousin, I wouldn't need to break up with him, huh?"

Okay, dumb question. But I'd never seen lips as perfectly formed as hers. I cleared my throat. *Professionalism,* I reminded myself. "Um, I mean, is this his home address? I need to know so I can, uh, come up with a plan of attack."

She raised a skeptical eyebrow. "What do you charge?" she asked.

Now I was in familiar territory. "Twenty-five."

She pulled some money out of the driver's console and pushed it toward me. I glanced up the street to see if any cars were coming, but fortunately it was West Oak.

"Of course . . ." I started, but then thought better of it.

"What? You charge more to break up with a guy?"

"No, no, it's just that, well, sometimes . . ."

"Spit it out, junior."

Why do high-schoolers always have cute little names for kids younger than them?

"Well, I usually offer to include flowers and chocolates to, well, to let them down gently."

The girl stared at me for a moment and then laughed. "Flowers and chocolates. Oh, Duke would love that, wouldn't he?" She stared at me a little more. "What do you charge for that?"

"Another twenty-five."

She glanced at her friend and smirked. "Tell you what, junior. My little two-timer would enjoy those flowers and bon-bons just a little too much. But you go out and find yourself a dead rat. Wrap it up in a box, nice and pretty, and give it to him as a gift from me. You do that and I'll give you another twenty-five."

A dead rat. Right. I laughed, just a little. "That's a good one."

She stared right at me without a flutter of her long blond eyelashes. "I'm not joking, kid. I want a dead rat. Can you do that or do I need to take my business elsewhere?"

"Uh . . . no, no, not a problem. The Heartbreak Messenger can handle anything you want." I didn't need her creating competition for me over a dead rodent. The rat idea was way too gross for my tastes, but at least there wouldn't be any big expenses.

"Good." She shoved some more money into my hands. "I need it done soon. By tomorrow." Then she pushed the gear shift and squealed into the other lane and down the street.

I double counted the money and shoved it into my pocket, next to the chump change from Mick's stamps. Fifty bucks, easy as pie. I looked around at the stores that lined the street. *Now where,* I wondered, *do they sell dead rats?*

Chapter 19

"Y ou need to find a what?" Rob looked at me as if I had suggested we run naked through the hallway. We were in PE, shooting hoops out on the asphalt courts. Rob and I had a backboard to ourselves. We weren't very good, so no one was dying to play with us.

"Yeah, I know, I know. It's pretty gross. But everybody has their own style. This is what she wants. Besides, she paid me for it."

"She paid you to give a dead rat to her boyfriend?"

"Hey, don't knock it, man. My clients have

been very satisfied so far." I shot and the ball flew at least a foot under the basket.

"Quentin, more follow-through," shouted Coach Wong. He moved his hand through the air like his wrist was broken. I waved and nodded. As if I knew what he was talking about.

Rob ran after the ball and came back dribbling. "That's just so cold, man. A dead rat."

"So, any idea where I can find one?" I had spent the previous evening looking around our apartment complex, hoping to find some rat traps, or at least a mouse. All I came up with was a fistful of dryer lint in the laundry room. I didn't want to admit it to Rob, but I was stressing out just a little. The girl in the Mustang didn't strike me as the understanding type. Her fifty dollars was on loan unless I could deliver a dead rat. And with the end of the month approaching, I needed that cash.

Rob looked at me in mock surprise. "The Great Heartbreak Messenger needs help? And here I thought you had all the answers." He tossed high and made it. Lucky shot.

"Why on earth would I know where to find a dead rat? I mean, do you?"

He grabbed the rebound. "I might have a few ideas."

"Oh, yeah? Like what?"

"A few ideas I might be persuaded to share . . ." He let his words hang in the air.

Oh, I saw how it was going to be. I considered Rob's offer as he tossed the ball up and swished it again. Another lucky shot. He grabbed the rebound and bounced it to me. "Fine, I'll give you five bucks if you help me find a dead rat," I said.

"No way. I want a cut of the deal."

A cut of the deal? What did Rob think we were? Gangsters planning a bank job? "Thanks, Rob. In that case I can find my own dead rat." I shot and missed, but I let my hand flap around a little more, just in case Coach Wong was looking.

Rob didn't move for the rebound. I turned and saw him staring at me, looking like I'd punched him in the gut.

"Come on," I said. "It's a dead rat, not a rare diamond. I'm still going to be doing the hard part. Five bucks is more than fair. And I could use your help."

Rob glanced around and finally shrugged. "Well, all right. If you need the help."

I smiled. "Cool. So what's your idea for finding a rat?"

"Quentin! Rob! This isn't basket weaving! Grab that ball and start practicing!"

♥ ♥ ♥

Our dead-rat expedition started as soon as the bell rang at the end of our last class. Rob and I headed down to the school basement. It was a small basement, more like an underground storage closet for cleaning supplies and the scenery from last year's theater production. It was also where the school custodian, Mr. Montgomery, had his office.

Mr. Montgomery didn't like kids much, and who would if you spent the day cleaning up after them? He didn't usually surface until most of the kids had left the school grounds. Some people said that he even slept in a bed in his office and brushed his teeth in the student bathrooms at night.

My eyes slowly adjusted to the dim light as we

descended the basement stairs. There was shelf after shelf of cleaning supplies and an army of mops. In a corner I saw the hand-painted trees from *The Wizard of Oz*. Rob only hesitated a second before walking up to Mr. Montgomery's office door and giving it a quick knock.

"Who is it?" barked a voice.

Rob looked at me. "Uh . . . Rob McFallen."

Silence for just a moment. "What? Did ya ralph in the hallway again?"

Even in the dim light of the basement, I could tell Rob's cheeks were flushed pink.

"Wow," I said under my breath. "He still remembers that?"

"Abby did it first," Rob muttered.

That was true. The year before, poor Abby had the stomach flu and threw up at school. You'll never see a crowd of kids scatter faster than when somebody pukes in the hall. While Abby went to see the nurse, the office lady sent Rob to get Mr. Montgomery. The janitor had grabbed a bucket of sawdust and mumbled to himself as Rob led him to ground zero. Then Mr. Montgomery made Rob hold the bucket as he sprinkled the sawdust over Abby's regurgitated lunch. The sight of the sawdust landing softly on the mess didn't do much for Rob's stomach, and he puked on top of it all.

Rob cleared his throat. "We just have a question for you, Mr. Montgomery."

There was another moment before the door swung open. Mr. Montgomery stood there in his usual blue coveralls, his scruffy gray beard scratching against the collar. "Well, start asking. I got work to do."

"Um . . ." Rob stared at Mr. Montgomery. I was afraid he was having flashbacks of sawdust on vomit, and I didn't want to think what that might do to his stomach. So I quickly stepped in.

"We're looking for rats. Preferably dead ones."

The school janitor stared at me like I'd just asked him for a dead rat.

"It's for a project. For biology class." I'm certainly not a chronic liar, but sometimes a harmless lie is so much easier than trying to explain the truth to someone who doesn't care to begin with.

"Rats," said Mr. Montgomery.

"Yeah," said my fearless comrade, who had found his tongue again. "We thought . . . well, it was my idea . . . but we thought you probably set traps for them. Have you caught any lately?"

"This school don't have a pest problem," Mr. Montgomery said flatly.

"Oh, come on," said Rob. "Everybody knows what they do in the school cafeteria. There's got to be . . ."

"This school don't have a pest problem."

"Not even one little rat?" I asked.

Mr. Montgomery folded his arms. "This school passes its semiannual inspection with a gold rating. It don't have a pest problem."

A movement on the floor made me look down. A big brown cockroach scurried past the janitor's boot. He followed my eyes and then immediately lifted his foot and slammed it down on the bug. It crunched beneath his boot. His arms were still folded.

"As I was saying, boys, I got work to do."

We reluctantly turned and headed back up the

stairs. As we reached the top, I glanced behind me and noticed Mr. Montgomery hadn't moved.

Once we were back in the bright fluorescent lights of the hallway, Rob looked at me and shrugged. "Plan B?"

I nodded. "Plan B."

Chapter 20

→

For the Birds was a bit of a ride from the junior high, but it was the only pet store in town. We pulled up onto the curb and left our bikes next to the entrance. As I moved to open the door, Rob glanced into an uncovered metal trash can set in the sidewalk. His hand shot out to pull me backward. "Hey, take a look at this."

He reached into the trash can and pulled out a box the size of a video game console. It was pink with a white illustrated ribbon wrapped around it. The words "A gift for you . . ." were written in girly cursive across the lid.

"What do you think?" Rob asked.

"I don't think it's your color," I said, still holding the pet shop door handle.

"No. I mean, it's just the right size. Don't you think?"

"Rob, you pulled it out of the trash. It smells like perfume and . . . cheeseburgers."

It was hard to miss the triumph in his smile. "What are you going to do? Put the dead rat in your pocket?"

I hadn't thought that far ahead. "Good point. Bring it along."

A bell dinged once as we opened the door and a whole array of unusual smells were crammed up my nose. Despite its name, Rob was sure the store had all sorts of animals. With the variety of odors that greeted us, I figured he was right.

A young man behind the counter looked up from his magazine and pushed his glasses farther up his nose. "Hello, there!"

I nodded, looking at the animal cages as I walked past. Lots of birds. Lizards. Hamsters, or gerbils. Fish. Small snakes. And a tarantula.

"What can I do for you guys?" the man behind the counter asked eagerly.

I glanced at Rob and decided I'd better do the talking this time. "Do you carry rats?"

"Sure do." The man walked over to the side wall and lifted a small steel cage from one of the higher shelves. He brought it back and set it on the counter. "These, my friends, are hooded fancy rats. Still very young, but a good size."

I crouched down and peered in the cage. It held two rats, both of them taking tentative steps. Their noses twitched at the edge of the cage. Their bodies were white, and it looked as though the tops of their heads had been dipped in chocolate.

"Both males, both very healthy," the man continued.

Hmmm. Where to go from there . . . "This is kind of a weird question, but have you had any rats die on you lately?"

The man suddenly looked concerned. "No. Have you? Is something going around?" He pulled the cage back a little bit, as if I was going to sneeze on it.

"No, no. It's just that, well . . . we're looking for a dead rat."

"Your rat died?"

"No. I've never had a rat."

"Then whose dead rat are you looking for?"

"No one's. We just happen to be looking for a dead rat."

"Well, I don't carry those. I keep all of my animals *alive*."

"What about snakes?" Rob chimed in. "Big ones. Don't you keep dead animals around to feed big snakes?"

The man shook his head. "Most big snakes will eat dead mice." He glanced nervously at the other cages on the wall. "*Frozen* dead mice. I don't carry any, but I can order some for you, if you like."

"How long will they take to get here?" I asked.

"About a week."

I could feel Mustang Girl's deadline looming over my head. She wanted the job done today. I pictured the fifty dollars in my sock drawer disappearing at the stroke of midnight.

Rob suddenly snapped his fingers and pointed at the hooded fancy rats. "Hey. How much would one of those cost?"

The man pulled the cage all the way back so that it pressed against his body. "Fifteen dollars. Why?"

Rob looked at me and opened his eyes wide. He nodded slightly toward the cage. I knew what he was thinking. Fifteen dollars. Even with the five bucks I was paying him, that would still leave me thirty dollars' profit. Not great, but the clock was ticking.

But I also knew that a live rat wouldn't exactly carry the same message, and my client had been very specific. Which meant we would need to . . . well, bump off the rat. I leaned down and peered into the cage. One of the rats froze this time, staring at me. His whiskers twitched, sending a shudder through its soft furry body. His gleaming black eyes seemed to plead with me.

Now, I've never been much of an animal person. That's what you get for growing up in an apartment, I guess. But I don't exactly go around kicking dogs, either.

No worries, I silently told the hooded fancy rat. I stood up. "Thanks for your help. Let's go, Rob."

Rob held out his hands in exasperation. "Quentin, hold on. This is perfect."

I headed for the door. "Come on, Elmer Fudd. Leave the furry little animals alone."

If I didn't have the heart to take a pet rat hostage, then we needed to move on. Time was running out.

Chapter 21

Technically, we were now on Plan C, but we didn't feel right calling it that. Plan C implied that we had more plans in the playbook. But this one was it. If it didn't work I was sunk. Plan Hail Mary was more like it.

We rode our bikes all the way out past the edge of town to a fenced-off piece of land bigger than a football stadium. The massive chain-link fence had a single wide gate in the front with a purple-lettered sign that read JORGE'S SCRAP YARD. We parked our bikes and walked through the open gate.

We hadn't taken three steps inside when a massive black dog leaped out of nowhere, filling the air with resonating barks. I practically fell over myself trying to scramble out of biting range. Like I said, I'm not really an animal person. The dog's dark eyes fixed on mine and a fresh shot of drool sprayed out of its snarling tan muzzle with each bark. I don't know what kind of dog it was, but it sure looked like a cross between mean and ugly. Rob was halfway to his bike before I had a chance to blink, but as I scrambled I noticed the dog was on a chain. I took a breath and slowly stood with my hands out to show I was unarmed and peace loving. The dog settled down to a snarl, sniffed at a rock, and huffed at me.

When it became clear that I was no longer on the menu, I stood up straight and looked around.

Jorge's had a reputation in our corner of the state. When people needed to locate a hard-to-find piece of whatever, they came all the way out to the scrap yard. It was kind of like Disneyland for junk collectors. I'd only been here once before when Mom was trying to find an engine for a 1977 Camaro. The place was filled with dozens of crooked rows piled with scrap. Most of it was metal, a lot of it was from cars, but overall it was an impressive grab bag of junk. Given some time, I wouldn't have minded just wandering around to see what was there.

Off to the left stood a dirty white building with a tin roof. An oversized rocking chair made of rough wood took up most of the porch. And a round man with a thick mustache took up most of the rocking chair. I walked toward him, keeping one eye on the dog.

"This ain't a playground," the man barked. "Are you two paying customers?"

"We will be if we find what we need," I said. I wasn't going to be pushed around like a kid when I was on official business with a schedule to keep.

"What you looking for?"

"Um . . . we'll know it when we see it." After Plan A and Plan B, I was just a little reluctant to mention what we were really doing.

"Okay," said the man, who I assumed was Jorge. "Just be careful." He gestured to the dog behind me. "Barbados eats shoplifters. And don't break anything!" He laughed, and I got the feeling he made that joke a lot.

I turned and gave Barbados plenty of room as I walked the other way. The dog snarled in my direction. I gave him even more room. Rob was still standing with one leg over his bike. "The dog's tied up, Superman," I said. "Let's go. And grab the box."

Rob hesitated, eyes on the dog, and then untied the pink gift box from the back of his bike.

We walked down the nearest aisle of scrap, which stretched on for fifty yards before turning and merging into the next aisle, just like a supermarket. I heard the dog following us, but didn't pay it much attention. After a while, though, I began to wonder just how long his chain was, so I turned to look. The chain stretched back about twenty feet, but the other end wasn't attached to anything. I fought back a surge of panic and focused on looking as innocent as possible. Barbados growled deep in his throat.

Rob noticed me staring and glanced back. He snapped his head forward as his walk became stiff. "Quentin! You said that crazy dog was chained up!" he whispered, as though he didn't want the dog to know we were talking about him.

"Well, there's obviously a chain on him." I sounded a lot more confident than I felt. "Just act normal. I'm pretty sure dogs can smell fear."

"Exactly! And junkyard dogs eat it for breakfast."

"Maybe this one's a vegetarian. Listen, Rob, it's not going to eat a customer. Just act cool, don't steal anything, and it won't bother us." I forced myself to walk more casually to prove my point.

We moved on, stopping to look at the piles of junk now and then, but mostly casting sideways glances at the dog. It lost interest in us whenever we stopped, sniffing around the piles and looking for treasures of its own. Whenever we started forward again it perked up its ears and trailed behind us.

Rob seemed to relax a bit when it was clear that the dog didn't intend to eat us any time soon, and watching the seconds tick away quickly beat down any of my own canine phobias. "So, genius," I said. "Where do they keep the dead rats around here?"

I hated to admit it, but Rob's ideas for dead-rat hunting were pretty good, even though we hadn't struck carcass yet. He always had a knack for finding useless but interesting things. Like once in the fourth grade, Rob and I were walking behind the elementary school, back where the kitchen lets out. He saw something metal lying by the foundation of the building. It was a brass cylinder about the length of his finger, with all sorts of intricate carvings on it. We didn't know what it was, but it sure looked cool. It had a square hole at the top and Rob put a chain through it and wore it around his neck like a pendant. Everybody always stopped him on the playground to look at it.

Then one day vice principal Vandenburg saw it and pulled him aside. They talked quietly for a few minutes. Finally Rob reluctantly pulled the chain over his head and placed the pendant into her hand. When she walked off, I asked Rob what had happened. Apparently vice principal Vandenburg wanted to know where Rob had gotten the toilet handle from the teacher's restroom, and why he was wearing it around his neck.

I just hoped Rob's weird talent for unearthing junk would work today. And soon.

Rob scratched his head and surveyed the heaps surrounding us. "Well, you'd think in a place like this you'd be seeing big signs for rat hotels. Maybe that slobber machine back there scares them away. But if I were Jorge, and if I had a rat problem, I'd probably be setting out traps at every . . . oh, no way!" He stopped and stared into the pile of scrap off to the side. I tried to figure out what he was so excited about, but it all looked like junk to me.

"You have got to be kidding me!" He dove into the pile, climbing over a few toaster ovens and a lawnmower to pull up the corner of a road sign. He bent low to get a good grip on it, and then yanked upward. The sign must have been at least four feet from one corner to the other, and painted a bright reflective orange. Solid black lettering in the middle of the diamond spelled out DIP. Barbados growled again.

The sign was still connected to the pole that had once held it up, so Rob struggled a bit to pull it all out. The pole was slightly bent, probably from where a careless driver had brought an end to its boring existence.

"That's nice, Rob. But we're here to find rats."

"Are you kidding me? This is so much better than rats. This is . . . This is . . ." Rob was at a loss for words, which was a first, as far as I could remember.

"You really want a giant broken road sign that says DIP?" That presented more insult opportunities than I could even count, so I just let it go.

"Oh, come on, man. This is a once-in-a-lifetime find. I'm so glad I came along today. How much do you think that guy will charge for it?"

"If you're lucky, five bucks, since that's all the money you have right now."

Rob tucked one side of the road sign under his arm and started dragging the pole behind him. It made a horrible rocks-in-a-blender sound as the twisted metal end dragged against the gravel. Barbados seemed to like that. He barked at the metal pole and tried to gnaw at it. He yipped and skittered in circles around us like a puppy. Apparently he thought Rob had found him a giant junkyard chew toy.

Rob dragged that stupid sign for nearly an hour as we looked under dozens of pieces of junk for rat traps, or anything else that might indicate rodents. I told Rob to put the sign down, that we could come back for it later, but he was sure somebody else would take it the second he let it go. Somehow I didn't think two DIP sign collectors could show up at the same scrap yard at the same time. The world would probably self-destruct or something.

After an hour and a half Rob begged to take yet another break to give his arms a rest. "This thing is killing me, Quentin. I'm not going to have strength to do my chores when I get home. Not to mention my homework. You'll have to do it for me."

Homework. "Oh, man."

"What?"

"Abby was going to come study with us today."

"Abby? Is she back from the dead?"

"I ran into her yesterday. She said she needed our help."

"Ah . . . I'm touched. I wish I had my cell phone back. Hey, why don't we go see if Jorge has a phone and we can call her. Let her know we'll be late."

If we didn't show, she would write us off, I just knew it. Any chance I had of jump-starting our friendship again was being ripped to shreds and tossed into the wind. She had Justin. Why did she need friends that she couldn't even count on to help save her English grade?

Maybe Rob was right. There might still be time . . . but not enough for studying *and* for making fifty bucks.

"Rob," I said desperately, "the clock's ticking. It's going to be dark soon. I've got to find a dead rat, bike it all the way back to town, and go dump Duke Ripling before I can even start on my homework. I'm starting to feel a little stressed out here."

Rob was staring at me, as though I'd told him someone had already bought his DIP sign and was hauling it away at that very moment. "Did you say Duke Ripling?"

"Yeah. Why?"

"Duke Ripling who's going out with Lisa Monaghan?"

"I don't know. I guess so. Some girl named Lisa with a sweet silver Mustang."

Rob threw out his hands as if I was missing something.

"Duke Ripling, the king of the bench press? Duke Ripling, the first linebacker to ever be voted captain of the John P. Westmore high school football team? Duke Ripling, the guy that his teammates call Duke the Ripper? *That* Duke Ripling?"

My limited sports vocabulary was still processing the term "linebacker." I was pretty sure they were the really big guys that went to all-you-can-eat buffets just before a game.

"I think I'm gonna be sick," I said.

Barbados whimpered.

Rob somehow looked more scared than I was. He was probably concerned about who was going to help him with his homework after I got my brains beat out of me with a dead rat. "Don't worry, man," he finally said. "Maybe he wants to break up as much as she does."

I had my hands on my knees, staring at the ground, trying to breathe slowly. "Then why not give him a phone call instead of a dead rat?"

Rob thought a moment. "Maybe his hobby is taxidermy." Rob must have noticed my doubled-over, hyperventilating form, so he tried to change the subject. "Anyway, speaking of rats, let's get a move on. Hey, I know . . ." Rob gently walked toward the dog and clapped. "Good boy. Do you know how to find rats? Rats?"

Barbados was up on all fours.

Rob scrunched up his face and made whiskers around his nose with his fingers. "Rats?"

Barbados barked.

Rob scurried around, crouched down low, with finger-whiskers on his rat face.

"Rats? Yeah? Find the rats. Go find the rats, boy. Go! Find the rats! Go!"

Barbados tore off down the aisle of scrap, turning for a moment and barking for us to follow him. Rob looked at me and shrugged, then picked up his sign and started to run. I grabbed the other end so we could go faster.

Barbados went up to the end row, ran two rows over, and then down one, the chain whipping back and forth behind him. Halfway down, he came to a stop and barked like crazy, nose pointing to the scrap pile. We came up behind him and both stared at a metal garbage can lid lying flat on the ground. The dog scraped at it with his paw.

I looked at Rob. "You think?"

"Could be," he replied. Then he held up his hands and took a step back. "But it's *your* rat."

I looked around and found a golf putter. I carefully wiggled the putting end underneath the garbage can lid. I hesitated, wondering what was under there. If it was a live rat, I would have to be quick. Cute little hooded fancy rats were one thing, but a lean, mean junkyard rat was something entirely different.

With a single motion I flipped the can lid over and then raised the putter, ready to strike whatever was under there. Half a breath later, I dropped the putter, my hands flying to my nose and mouth.

"Ugh!" Rob said.

The stench was overwhelming. I took a few steps back before turning to look at what I had uncovered. I was stunned. Amazed. Absolutely speechless (and breathless) at the canine-produced miracle lying on the ground. Barbados had led us straight to a dead rat. Really dead. Roadkill-type dead. Dead-lying-under-a-hot-garbage-can-lid-all-day dead. Putrid-can't-breathe-because-the-smell-will-fry-your-brain dead.

And exactly the type of gift Mustang Girl probably had in mind.

But that wasn't going to happen. Not a chance. I wasn't about to touch that rat with a ten-foot pole, much less a three-foot putter. I wasn't going to strap that thing to the back of my bike, even in a box. I couldn't.

It took several minutes and twenty feet of distance before I could breathe clearly again. "There's no way, Rob," I said. "I'd gag and puke before I could even get out the message."

"I don't know, that might be a good thing. Duke would probably pass out, too, before he had a chance to kill you."

I seriously considered that for a minute. But, no. Not a chance.

"There's got to be something else. Something we haven't thought of." I turned to the dog. "Hey, boy. Another rat? Take us to another rat, boy!"

Barbados sat motionless. He looked at me under heavy dog eyebrows, seeming just a little annoyed. I groaned.

"Come on, Rob, think. What else can I do?"

"Well, she said a dead rat, but really it's the meaning she cared about right? Isn't there something else that sends the same message as, 'Hey, baby, our relationship means as much to me as this piece of roadkill? Hug hug, kiss kiss?' "

Again, Rob had a point. I was a messenger. It's what I did. If I substituted a dead rat with something equal, it would still get the point across. It was the end message that mattered, right? The client might not even find out. Maybe.

"Okay, so what else can we use?" I asked. "What can we find in the next fifteen minutes that's slightly more bearable than a decaying rat carcass?"

Suddenly there was another stench in the air, but this one was different. Gross, but more familiar. I glanced at Rob, who was looking at the dog, who was coming out of a squat. Rob grinned broadly. "You're just full of answers today, aren't ya, boy?"

I took a tentative breath, knowing that Rob, for too many times on the same day, was right. "Oh, crap," I said.

Chapter 22

Getting the dog poop scooped into the gift box was a little tricky, and Barbados growled at us a few times, but fortunately kept his distance. He seemed to sense how critical the situation was. I worried the guy at the front gate would want me to show him what was in the box. But Rob's DIP sign came to the rescue, since both Rob and the big guy were determined to get a good deal. They finally settled on seven dollars and fifty cents. Rob asked me if he could have the five I owed him, and then asked to borrow two-fifty. He said he'd started on the bucket of walnuts and would have the money to pay me back soon. I was pretty anxious to get out of there—the scrap heaps were already casting long shadows—so I forked over the money.

I strapped the gift box to the back of my bike. Rob laid the signpost across his lap and tried to balance it as he jammed down on his pedals. He kept one hand on the signpost and one hand on the handlebars and weaved back and forth as he picked up speed toward the road. He looked like an old-time tightrope walker about to plummet to a broken neck. I shook my head and followed.

It was slow going on the way back to town. Rob had a hard time balancing both his bike and the DIP sign. Once he tipped the balance of the sign and it dropped to the ground, scattering sparks across the asphalt. Once he tipped his own balance and careened into a ditch. After the second car passed us with its horn blaring, I rode up within earshot.

"Rob, let me take one end of the sign," I shouted.

He came to a stop and shook his head. "Go on without me, man. I'm slowing you down and you've got a thing to do."

I didn't want to leave him there alone with his

trapeze act, but time was short. "All right. Thanks. Should I swing by your place and tell Marcus to come pick you up?"

"No, I'm . . . Oh! Marcus. That's right." He tipped the sign to the ground and dug into his jeans pocket. "He gave me a note for you." Rob pulled out a crumpled piece of notebook paper and handed it to me.

I grabbed it and shoved it into my shirt pocket. Whatever Marcus had lined up for me next would have to wait until this job was in the bag. "Thanks, Rob. Don't get run over by a semi."

"Ha! You're in more danger of that than I am."

He didn't have to say the words—the feeling of dread was already wedged in my stomach like a fruitcake. I knew I was probably pedaling furiously toward my doom, but there was still the money to think about. No delivery, no money. No money, no apartment. The thought of our stuff sitting out on the curb spurred me on.

It took awhile to get back to civilization. I stopped at the garage for a minute to let Mom know what I was up to. Well, to let her know I was working on a "project" and would be back for dinner.

If I was still conscious. I didn't get off my bike, and I didn't let Mom get too close, since the client's dead-rat substitute was starting to stink outside the box.

Next I rode over to the Windy Terrace neighborhood. I wandered up and down the narrow streets filled with mobile homes, looking for the address that Lisa had given me. I finally found it, a small rectangular house with a neat flower bed in front—a perfect place to lay my body to rest once Duke was through with me.

As I unstrapped the gift box and left my bike on the front lawn, my hands were shaking. *Professionalism*, I told myself. *Just doing my job. For fifty bucks.*

I took a deep breath, cleared my throat, and knocked on the hollow wooden door with a trembling fist. A woman's voice called out, " 'Round back."

I walked past the corner of the trailer and found a back porch. A woman with scraggly pepper gray hair sat on the stairs. Lines hung under her eyes and she looked a lot older than my mom. She wore a uniform, maybe from a hospital or a restaurant, and a glowing cigarette dangled from her fingers.

The woman glanced up at me with tired eyes. "You looking for my Duke?" she asked.

I nodded, fingering the stinky gift box nervously. The woman shoved her cigarette into a flowerpot full of sand and brown butts, and then grabbed the stair railing and carefully hoisted herself up. She opened the back door. "Duke, someone looking for you," she called out in a husky voice. She gave me a last glance, and then slipped into the house.

The door opened a minute later and a head with auburn hair poked out. Duke stepped onto the small wooden porch, an almost-smile on his face. "Hey. Did you bring my new cleats?" His voice was deep and resonated like a bear's voice might, if it wore shoulder pads and was a senior in high school.

I shook my head, a little tongue-tied. Duke was immense. At least six-foot-eight and . . . well, who knows. Big. Refrigerator big. The stainless-steel Maytag kind with two doors that open side-by-side. The pink gift box felt slippery in my sweaty hands.

Duke nodded, as though showing me he understood something perfectly. "Well, okay, but let's do it quick. I've got some math homework tonight that's killing me."

Huh?

Did he know I was coming? Had he known his girlfriend was going to dump him? Using a seventh-grader? Was he almost-smiling because he knew, as a consolation, he would at least get to practice tearing someone apart limb from limb?

"You know why I'm here?" I croaked, readying myself for the first blow.

"Well, yeah. Same reason the other kids come."

I kind of doubted that.

"Um, Mr. Ripling . . ."

"Call me Duke." He pulled a Sharpie from his pocket and reached toward me, gesturing to the gift box. I yanked it away but his whole muscular body seemed to keep extending until I couldn't pull it away any farther. He took the box and looked at it for a moment. "A gift, huh? A superstar autograph will add a nice touch." He pulled the cap off his pen with his teeth and signed the box lid with a flourish that seemed carefully practiced.

He shoved the box back into my hands and capped his pen. "You can tell her that'll be worth a ton when I'm named an NFL MVP. Anyway, seeya, champ."

My target turned and headed back up the narrow stairs, pausing for a moment to glance at the soles of his shoes.

"Whoa, Duke, uh, hold on a minute. Please." The words tumbled out. I caught my breath, afraid that I might sound a little too chummy. His head swung back around on his telephone-pole neck and he looked at me. His almost-smile was gone.

I pushed through the lump in my throat and kept going. "Uh, the autograph's really great, and, I mean, thanks a lot. But I'm here to talk with you about something."

He didn't move. As motionless as a rock. Seriously. He eyed me the same way he might stare at the other linebacker, or whatever you call the dead duck on the other side of the line of scrimmage.

I am about to die.

I cleared my throat. "I have a message for you. From Lisa."

His hand fell to his side. The door slammed

shut. He turned slowly, no longer looking at me like I was just some little kid.

"You're him, aren't you?" The bearlike resonance was gone. His voice was hollow.

It was the same hopeless look Goat Girl had given me, with just a little more violence behind it. "You're the Heartbreak Messenger. And Lisa sent you."

Suddenly his face flushed red. His jaw trembled. His fists clenched. An ugly cry came from his throat, something barbaric and animal. His eyes fell on the large ashtray flowerpot sitting at the top of the stairs. He picked it up like a pebble and hefted it above his head. I stumbled backward as it crashed down a few feet in front of me on the cement driveway. Dirt and cigarette butts and shards of pottery poured across my shoes. Adrenaline pumped through my veins and I scrambled, ready to tear around the corner of the house and put some distance between us.

I glanced at him once more, expecting to see him lunging for my neck. And just as my eyes met his, the anger drained from his face and he collapsed. Like his muscles had given out. He crumpled onto the top step, his arms on his knees and his forehead on his arms.

And then Duke Ripling, a grizzly bear from the turf of manly men, cried like a baby.

Heaving sobs. And big, wet, slobbery sniffs. His body shook as he cried. He didn't hold back—maybe he couldn't. I'm sure the neighbors must have heard something. But he went on and on, like a storm.

My job was finished. Message delivered. The result may have even surprised my client. She probably would have liked to hear about it. All I had to do was place the autographed gift box at his feet and say, "Tough game, champ. Better luck next season."

But I couldn't. Just like with Goat Girl. I simply couldn't walk away from someone that was, well, blubbering. This was just a little different than Goat Girl, though. She was cute. She was a girl. A damsel in distress. This was an ogre.

I took a few steps toward him and waited for a reaction. When none came, I walked carefully up to Duke and sat next to him on the stairs. The storm was tapering off now. More snotty sniffles and less sobs. I put the gift box on the stairs, off to the side, and waited. I didn't think the situation really called for a hug. Footballers were probably more into head butting or something, anyway.

Finally he lifted his head. His eyes were puffy and glistening. He wiped the tears from his cheeks. He took a few shaky breaths. He wiped his nose with his shirt collar.

"Sorry you had to see that, Heartbreaker," he finally said. "I guess you're probably used to it by now."

I nodded vaguely. "It's all right, man. You gotta let it out."

He sighed, and then spoke some more, his voice still weak. "I saw this coming, you know? I tried to stop her, to make her understand, but she just wouldn't listen. She thinks I'm two-timing her, but that ain't the case. It's something I had to do."

I seemed to remember Lisa saying something about that offense.

"If I don't get my math grades up, I can't play. Coach told me that. The principal's not giving any exceptions. So I'm working on it, you know? I find a tutor, a junior girl, a nice kid that's real smart. Of course I have to spend some time with her. How else am I going to get my grades up, man? But it wasn't anything, she's a friend, she's helping me out. That's it. End of story."

"Have you talked with Lisa about it?" I asked.

Duke looked up at the stars, which seemed especially bright. "Lisa won't listen. She only sees what she wants. Not what's in here." He tapped his chest. "In here, it's all about her. No one else."

The neighborhood was silent, as if everyone was mourning in honor of Duke the Ripper. I looked over at that giant on the stairs next to me. He looked sincere. He looked like he was in pain. I wondered if his story was true, if he really did only have feelings for Lisa, and if she just blew off a guy that was completely and totally devoted to her.

"I'm sorry," I said. And I was. Not sorry that I'd delivered the message. That was just business, after all. Right? But I did feel sorry for him, that it all had to happen. Seemed like a little communication could have cleared things up. A different kind of communication.

Duke wiped his eyes again. "It's all good, dude. Thanks for listening. You're all right, Messenger."

He held out his fist. I tapped my fist down on his, and he did the same to mine. He looked up at the stars again, and then sniffed like he was smelling something and scrunched his eyebrows.

"Hey, kid, I think you must have dog poo on the bottom of your shoe."

Chapter 23

When I left Duke's house later that evening, I was still carrying the gift box full of dog crud. I didn't have the heart to leave it with Duke. Instead, I tossed it into the neighborhood Dumpster before hitting the road.

There was one more stop I had to make, even though it was well past dinnertime. A few blocks from my apartment, I parked my bike in the driveway of a one-story house with a tidy yard. I knocked on the door.

I heard the scurry of feet and then a curtain was whisked aside behind a glass panel in the door. The round black eyes of Katie, Abby's little sister, peered out at me for a brief second.

"Abby!" her muffled voice echoed. "There's a boy here for you. The one that's *not* your boyfriend."

I glanced up, pretending a sudden interest in the current phase of the moon.

The door opened a moment later. Abby peaked her head around the edge of the door. "Yes?" she asked with thin lips.

"Hey, Abby. Um, how's it going?"

"How's it going? Oh, fine. Just fine. Despite the fact that I beat my head against a picnic table all afternoon trying to get through my English homework alone."

"Yeah. Hey, we're really sorry about that. We got caught up in a project that took us all the way out to Jorge's Scrap Yard." I mentally braced myself for the cross-examination headed my way.

"Mmm-hmm. A project. What kind of project?" Somehow the question sounded like an accusation.

Tread carefully, man. "It was a . . . research project."

"Mmm-hmm. A research project. Did you find what you needed?"

"Yeah, but it took us awhile. Obviously."

Abby studied my eyes. Scrutinized them. I felt like a blob of gunk in a petri dish. "You know," she said, "the whole time I was sitting at that table— *alone*—I told myself that if you had stood me up to go off and break somebody's heart, that I wouldn't talk to you for a very, very long time. At least 'til next Presidents' Day. You weren't doing Heartbreak Messenger stuff, were you?"

Don't answer! Avoid the question. "Abby, we went to the scrap yard, just me and Rob. There aren't many hearts out there that need breaking. Just rats and junkyard dogs. All right?"

She scrutinized me some more.

"Hey," I said, "I'm here now, aren't I? I came straight to your house. I haven't even had dinner yet."

Abby turned off her scrutinizing rays, although she seemed reluctant to do it. "I know. Which is why, if you and Rob are lucky, I may grace you with my presence later this week."

I gave her a mock bow. "We would be honored."

"I'm doing some stuff with Justin, and I have my photography class tomorrow . . . so hopefully I don't get caught up in any *projects*. Good night, Mr. Chinetti." I saw her dimple flash just before she closed the door.

As I turned away, I felt pretty lucky. It's not every night you face both a bear and a wildcat—and come away without a scratch.

Now that the day was over, I rode slowly to Mick's, weaving my bike on and off the sidewalk under the streetlights. The experience with Duke Ripling kept replaying in my mind. I tried to push it aside, but it nagged at me, like a piece of popcorn stuck in my teeth. It had been a good job. Fifty bucks, minus the five for Rob and the extra two-fifty I loaned him that I'd probably never get back. I had come away without a black eye, with all my bones still intact, and with just a little cigarette ash dusting my shoe.

And yet, for the first time since starting my brilliant entrepreneurial scheme, I felt something I'd worked hard to avoid. Guilt.

I'd told myself a hundred times since leaving Duke's back porch that nothing was my fault. It wasn't my fault Duke was failing math. It wasn't my fault Duke had chosen a cute junior girl as a math tutor instead of some pimply nerd from the trigonometry club. It wasn't my fault his girlfriend was being unreasonable and had chosen to cold-heartedly end their relationship through some kid who was quickly becoming a legend. Not my fault in the least.

But there was the guilt, hanging around as if looking for a buddy. And I couldn't figure out why.

I pulled up to the garage bays at Mick's and popped the kickstand. Across the bay I could see Mom scrubbing her hands with the orange pumice soap. It was her early night, and she was getting ready to leave. She didn't notice me. I hung back, just watching, thinking about how starved I was.

Then, next to the stainless steel sink, she did something that I'd seen only once—maybe twice—before. And a few pieces of my mental puzzle clicked together.

Mom never wastes any time talking about my dad. She doesn't wallow in self-pity and let everyone know how much her life stinks. She never wishes things were different. At least, not out loud. But as I watched, she rinsed the scratchy orange soap from her hands, and dried them, the black crescent moons still under her fingernails. Then she pulled out two rings from her pocket. One was a silver ring I'd given her for Christmas, the other was a ring she'd had since high school. She slowly placed one of the rings onto the ring finger of her left hand and then held it out. She looked at it wistfully, as though it lay behind a glass case in a jewelry shop.

It was just for a moment. Then she moved the ring to the other hand and turned off the light by the sink.

And I realized that's where the guilt came from. Knowing that my dad, in his own way, was a heartbreaker, too.

Chapter 24

The day after my visit to Duke's, I sat at the picnic table at the end of the poplar path next to Mick's. Abby was at her weekly photography workshop with her mom. Rob had gotten detention for dozing off in Mr. Hogan's history class. And I was contemplating the best way to flee the country.

Mexico's closer, I thought to myself, *but I don't know Spanish. Why did I decide to take German this year instead of Spanish? Dummkopf! I could do Canada, but that would be one heck of a bike ride.*

I stared down at the crumpled piece of notebook paper lying on my open algebra textbook. The note Rob had given me after the scrap yard.

For the hundredth time I reread the words written in Marcus's sloppy handwriting.

Q—Gunner is asking around for you. Watch your back.

Gunner. The Beast. Leather jacket. Switchblade. Smile like a lion.

He's figured it out. He knows it was me. Panic clawed at me from the inside. *Why on earth did I try to take on a high-schooler like Gunner? What was I thinking?*

I took a deep breath, then let it out. Then another breath. *Don't jump to conclusions. Maybe he doesn't know. Maybe he just wants to ask if I've seen his black book. Maybe he found another girlfriend and wants to dump her already. He said he could be my best customer.*

I tried to push away the idea of Gunner hunting me down. I tore up the note and shoved the pieces into my pocket. I pulled out a pencil and stared at the numbers in my textbook. Pneumatic wrenches whirred inside the garage bays, and I tried not to let my mind morph the sound into the growl of a motorcycle.

I forced myself to plunge into a sea of variables, to think of something else.

$3a + 4b = 17$. Both a and b are whole numbers. What do they equal?

Eventually my mind relaxed and started to wander. Before I knew it I was jotting down a different set of numbers. Twenty-five for Melissa. Fifty for Carmen, minus fifteen for flowers and chocolates. Thirty for Ty's girl. What was her name? Oh. LaTisha. Thanks to her I'd had nightmares for a week about my hand being stuck between the jaws of a sewer gator.

I listed and totaled, thinking about the wad of cash pushed into an argyle sock in my drawer, and about Mom paying rent in a few days. I'd earned a little less than two hundred dollars—not bad for a part-time business owner trying to keep up with school and all—although I'd been hoping to pay at least half of the rent. Maybe there was still time.

I tried to picture the look Mom would have on her face when I casually walked into the kitchen and plopped down a couple hundred bucks. I'd pull an orange juice from the fridge, take a swig, and say, "That's for the rent. Just trying to do my part, you know?"

"Hey, Quentin. What's up?"

My head snapped up and my body tensed. Justin Masterson came toward me through the parking lot, his slight-but-annoying swagger scuffing the cement. The air suddenly smelled like hair gel. I relaxed a little. At least it wasn't Gunner.

I turned a page in my textbook, suddenly very interested in variables. "Nothing. Abby's not here."

"Yeah, I know. At some class with her mom."

Yeah, and actually, it's a photography workshop down at the community center she goes to every Wednesday from three to five, I added silently. I scribbled an answer for number ten on my homework.

Justin sat down across the table from me. I glanced at him, and then copied number eleven out of the book.

"Algebra, huh?" he said. "That stuff can be

killer. Trying to keep all those variables straight. Figure out which one means what. And then you change one of them, and suddenly everything else changes with it."

I shrugged. "It's not bad."

Justin let the silence hang there for a moment before speaking again. "You know, there sure are a lot of people talking about you these days."

My heart skipped a beat. I scribbled something, anything, on my scratch paper. I didn't look up. "About me? You must have the wrong Quentin."

"Don't be so modest. Every rumor I hear floating down from the high school is about that Heartbreak Messenger. He's got quite the business going. Smart guy."

I erased what I'd written and brushed the rubber dust away, biting my tongue. I certainly wasn't going to let him draw me out with flattery.

"I know it's you."

I stopped writing. I knew it would work its way into the junior high eventually. I didn't exactly wear a mask and spandex when I did a job. All it would take is a former customer pointing at me as I walked past in the supermarket, saying to his junior-high sister, "Hey, that dude's the Heartbreak Messenger." And Rob knew, which meant all of creation would find out before Thanksgiving. I just didn't think Abby would be the one to spill the beans, especially to Polo-shirt Boy.

"I didn't hear it from Abby, by the way, if she even knows."

The mention of her name made me look up. "Of course she knows." I couldn't resist saying it like only a best friend could.

"It took some serious investigation to find out your secret identity." He looked at me expectantly.

"And what makes you so curious?"

He glanced off into the swaying poplars. "I've got a job for you."

"Who? Your sister?" I knew he had a sister in high school.

He laughed, short and quick. "No." He cleared his throat. "Me."

It took a moment for my algebra-drenched brain to catch up. "You don't mean . . ."

"Yeah. Abby."

Something rushed through my body like a

gust through the trees. I felt like pumping my fist back and forth and whooping. I felt like doing a crazy victory dance in the end zone. I felt like slapping Justin on the back and shouting, "Yes, yes, yes! You better believe I'll take the job!"

And then I stopped and wondered why I felt that way. Justin started talking again before I found an answer.

"I know Abby's your friend and all . . ."

Best friend, actually. One of two.

". . . but I thought that might actually make it easier to, you know, deliver the message." Justin didn't look up. Instead he picked at a few bits of lint on his shirt.

I nodded. "Why don't you want to break up with her yourself?" The question took me by surprise. I couldn't believe I'd said that to a customer ready to fork over money.

Justin looked at me, his swagger showing in his eyes. He gestured to my books on the table. "Algebra just seems like numbers and letters until you get into it. Then you realize that it's actually pretty complicated. Breaking up's not as easy as it sounds, either. When it's your own girlfriend, I mean. I'm sure you'll understand someday. But if you're not comfortable doing it, I can probably find someone else. . . ."

Images flashed through my mind. Goat Girl weeping like a broken pipe. LaTisha angry and hurt. Duke the Ripper blubbering. Abby crying painful tears . . . and then me, her best friend, waiting with open arms. Me comforting her in a time of need. Me telling her what a jerkwad that ex-boyfriend is and how she's totally better off without him. Me, with my old friend back.

"I'll do it," I said. "I was just curious, that's all. I'd never turn down a paying customer that needs a hand." Especially this customer.

He asked the price. I told him.

He'd heard about the flowers and the chocolates. I put him down for both.

He wanted it done as soon as possible. I said I'd take care of it.

Then Justin thanked me, turned, and sauntered away like a guy without a care in the world.

Thoughts sprang into my head one on top of another. Abby would be around to laugh with again. We could start doing our homework together everyday, just like old times. We could go look for shooting stars whenever we wanted. She and Justin together never made sense anyway. She would be so much happier without him.

I closed my algebra book and folded my arms.

She'll probably take it hard at first. Perhaps a few tears, a few curses to the gods of love. Then she'll be ready for comfort. A firm shoulder to cry on. Strong arms to hold her. She'll need her friends right by her side.

There was one minor thought, however, that I kept pushing to the back of the line.

Abby was about to get dumped by her boyfriend—and her best friend was going to deliver the message.

And there was that guilt again.

Chapter 25

- - - ➤

That evening I stared at the phone for over an hour. Alone in our apartment, I knew I had to do it. Pick it up. Dial the number. Set things in motion. It had to be done.

I needed a fixed time. An appointment. Abby might come by for homework the next day, but then she might not. I could wait until class, but there was always the possibility that I might not get to talk with her. Or I might get the chance, but then chicken out, turning yellow in the few seconds it took to walk up to her and say . . .

I picked up the handset.

I put it down.

This will be good for her. Justin's a bigheaded know-it-all. She deserves better. I'm doing this for her.

I picked it up, then put it down.

Sigh. *And for fifty bucks.*

I picked it up and dialed her number.

It rang. It rang again. I fought the urge to jam my finger into the red OFF button.

"Hello?" an adult voice answered.

"Hi. Is Abby there?"

"Sure, Quentin, hold on."

I counted seconds to calm my nerves. One Mississippi. Two Mississippi. Three Miss . . .

"Hey, Quentin. What's up?"

Okay. That was a much friendlier greeting than I'd expected after standing her up the other night. I swallowed over the lump in my throat. "Hey, Abby. How are you?"

"Fine. Playing Monopoly with Katie. Getting my trash kicked."

"Cool. Um, hey, can you come by Mick's tomorrow after school? There's some things I want to run by you."

Some things I want to run by you? Was I nuts?

Couldn't I at least prepare her for the nuclear bomb I was going to drop?

Pause. She finally said, "I was planning to come by for homework anyway."

"Okay. Cool."

"Assuming you guys are actually going to be there this time, instead of off ruining people's lives."

I bit my tongue and managed to say, "Don't worry. We'll be there."

"What kinds of things did you want to run by me?"

Tears. Heartache. Freedom. "Just some things. I'll tell you tomorrow. See you then."

"Um, okay. See you . . ."

I hung up before she even finished her good-bye.

Abby was in place.

But there was still Rob. If he showed up, who knew how the delivery might turn out? The next day at school I told him there were things I needed to take care of that afternoon.

"What kind of things?" he asked.

"Just some things."

His face darkened. "Oh. Heartbreak Messenger things, huh?"

I hesitated. Rob didn't like Justin much, either, but I knew the whole thing would be easier if I handled it myself.

"Oh, come on, Rob. Don't be a baby."

"Me? You're the one who'd rather spend time with sobbing females than your best friend."

I rolled my eyes and pulled out a five-dollar bill from my pocket. "Go over to Holey Doughs after school and buy a box. I'll meet you at your house when I'm done with business."

Rob glared at me for a moment longer, recognizing my bribe for what it was. Then he snatched the money from my hand. "Thanks. But you'd better not take too long. One of your doughnuts will die a horrible death each hour until you arrive."

"Fair enough." Holey Doughs was across town— and well worth the trip—which would keep Rob busy most of the afternoon.

I made my rounds as soon as school let out. I bought the standard box of chocolates, mostly because I knew Abby didn't really eat a lot of chocolate, so no use wasting money on the good stuff.

As I tucked the box under my arm, I wondered if Justin knew she didn't eat much chocolate. *Probably not.* For the flowers I bought the regular white carnations. The lady at Pretty Bouquets tried to talk me into getting some nicer flowers, roses or something, but I didn't want Justin to get more credit than he deserved.

And then it was time.

She wasn't at the picnic table when I got to Mick's, but I could see someone in the poplar trees, on the wooden bridge that spanned across the stream. I recognized Abby's blond hair falling down past her shoulders. I took a deep breath and started toward the poplar path, holding the flowers and chocolates behind my back.

I'd spent the rest of the previous evening trying to figure out a good one-liner that I could open with that might soften the blow. I'd even looked through my mom's Chicken Soup for the Soul books hoping to find a winner, but came up empty. I was going to have to wing it.

Abby heard me coming. She gave me a slow, absentminded glance, and then turned back around to stare at the stream.

"Hey, Quentin."

Maybe the sun had blinded her, or maybe she was just lost in thought. Either way she didn't seem to notice anything out of the ordinary. I came up beside her, still keeping the goods out of sight. Somehow I felt like I was about to commit a felony.

"What you up to?" I asked.

"Just thinking."

"About what?"

"Justin."

"Oh." My voice cracked a little.

She glanced at me again and I turned my body toward her to keep things out of sight. "Lately I've been so worried about him, about us," she said. "He's been getting upset at the stupidest things. And I was sure it was my fault, you know? But today he was totally different. So happy. We had the best conversation at lunch."

"Oh? What did you talk about?" For a moment I wondered if Justin had laid a few hints for her about what was hidden behind my back.

Abby laughed. "His pet turtle. He got a ball for his turtle to play with, but whenever Justin drops the ball into its cage, the turtle just pulls inside its shell. I told him he needed to get a dog instead."

Their last conversation together and they talked about pet turtles. Justin was even more of a wimp than I thought.

"Anyway," Abby said, "hopefully he's gotten over whatever's been bothering him and things will be back to normal."

I didn't say anything. I couldn't. It was the perfect chance to jump in with, "Well, actually, Justin's definition of 'normal' is a little different than yours." Or at the very least I could have shaken my head sadly. But I just stood there, wide-eyed and tongue-tied.

She must have sensed something because she glanced at me and then did a double take. "What's the matter, Quentin?" She suddenly noticed the way I was standing. She craned her neck to see what was behind my back. There was a half smile on her lips, like she expected me to yell, "Surprise!"

"What's going on?"

I opened my mouth like a wooden puppet, but no sound came out. The words were wedged deep in my throat and refused to budge. They had come for Melissa and Carmen and Goat Girl and Duke the Ripper, but the one person that I really cared about, the one person I knew so well, I just couldn't say them to her.

I didn't have to. They were written on my face with black permanent marker. Abby's half smile faded. She took a step away from me. I let my hands fall to my sides, exposing the dreaded tokens of the Heartbreak Messenger. "Oh, no," she whispered. She looked into my eyes, pleading so hard that it hurt, and I had to glance away.

"He wouldn't do that to me."

"I'm sorry." I croaked out the words.

"He wouldn't do that to me," she whispered again.

And then, as though she'd just thought of something, her expression seemed to crumple with even more pain. Or maybe that was just my imagination. But the words she spoke were real. "*You* wouldn't do that to me." Her eyes glistened with reluctant tears. One escaped and tore a wet line down her face.

"Abby, I . . ."

"My boyfriend *paid* my best friend to break

up with me. Now who's shoulder am I supposed to cry on?" For a minute she looked like she was going to hit me, or try to toss me over the bridge. But she didn't. She turned, more tears blazing trails down her cheeks, and ran up the poplar path.

"Abby! Wait!" I hurried after her. There was so much to say. So much to explain. So much comfort I was supposed to be giving. I sprinted through the trees.

Abby stopped abruptly and whirled around. "You stay away from me, Quentin! I don't need you anymore."

The words slapped my face, and then backhanded it again, just to be sure. I watched her run away, disappearing into the trees.

I couldn't breathe. I'd only run for a few seconds, but it felt like someone was sitting on my chest. The trees spun around me. I stumbled back toward the bridge.

I don't know how dirt feels. But if it feels the way I did at that moment, I don't know how it lives with itself. One thing I do know is this: In the end, the Messenger's heart got broken just like everyone else's.

Chapter 26

I stood at the bridge for a long time, staring into the water. At one point I must have opened up the package of chocolates and eaten some, because when I looked down later, only the ones with nuts were left. I pried my tired elbows off the bridge railing and made my way toward the garage in the twilight.

Mom was working on a Ford Taurus. Looked like a water pump problem. I laid the flowers on the air compressor next to the car as I walked past.

"Hi, Quentin." She looked at the flowers. "Are these for me?"

"No," I said as I pulled two microwavable

pizzas out of the freezer. I stuck them both into the microwave, one on top of the other. I walked by again and laid the half-eaten chocolates next to the flowers. "Neither are these. But you can have them, too."

She looked at them, then at me. "These aren't European, are they?"

I didn't answer. I walked to the garage bay door and stared out at the evening.

"Well, at least you left me the nuts."

She wouldn't say anything else. She never did. She never pried.

When the pizzas were done, I sat down and waited for her to slide into the chair across from me.

"Your turn," she said.

I took a bite of pizza. The cheese burned my mouth, but I kept chewing. The crust was thin and floppy. "Breaking up," I said quietly.

Mom nodded, unfazed. "All right. You wanna start?"

Apparently I did. Because before I knew it, my whole story came out. I started with Marcus McFallen at his house, and how the Heartbreak

Messenger name appeared from nowhere and just stuck to me. I told her the truth about the "bathroom sink" my face ran into. I told her about wanting to help out with the rent, about goats and the girl in the sweet Mustang, about digging with Rob through the stacks of scrap. (She found the dead rat and the dog poop incredibly funny.) I told her about all the messages in between. I even told her about Abby, about how I'd ruined her life and how she'd probably never speak to me again. I told her just about everything (except for Gunner's knife and the note from Marcus—some things you just don't tell your mom).

"Well," she said after she'd finished her pizza and I'd hardly touched mine. "Sounds like you've been busy. And it sounds like you've been making bank. You've really been doing this just to help out with the rent?"

I nodded, and then stopped myself, knowing I couldn't lie to my mom, not tonight at least. "Well, I've been telling myself that over and over. And I do want to help with the rent. But to be honest, I probably would have done it even if I hadn't overheard your phone call. People respect the Heartbreak Messenger. He has power. I guess I've kinda liked that."

Mom studied my face with a quiet smile. "I'm glad I wasn't the only motivation behind it. I hate to tell you, Quentin . . . well, no, I'm happy to tell you . . . we don't have rent problems. I make enough here at Mick's and that isn't going to change anytime soon."

The events of the day were suddenly put on pause as I tried to understand her words. "But I heard you . . ."

"You heard part of a conversation I had with your Uncle Ethan." She glanced over her shoulder. "I've been kicking around the idea of opening up my own garage. You know, starting my own business. I dragged Ethan into it just to get a second opinion. But the bottom line is that I'd never be able to get a loan big enough. Even if I could find a vacant building in a good location, the rent alone would shut us down. It was just an idea, so it's no big deal. But that's what I was discussing on the phone."

I tried to rewind my memory and replay the overheard conversation in this new light. "You mean we don't have problems paying the rent?"

She shook her head. "Not even a microproblem."

"What about the electric bill?"

"I'm terrible with remembering to pay bills on time. That certainly wasn't my first late notice."

My mind whirled. I wasn't sure whether to be upset that I'd worried so much about that for nothing, or to be happy that I still had oodles of cash stored away that did *not* need to be used for rent.

Mom reached over and held my chin in her hand. "But I think it is so sweet that you have a roll of bills saved up in your sock drawer just to help us out. You're a good person, Quentin."

I sighed. "Good people don't hurt their friends, especially not their best friends." I looked into Mom's soft brown eyes. "Do you think I've ruined things? Do you think Abby will ever speak to me again?"

"Hmmm . . ." Mom leaned back in her chair and folded her arms. "How long have you two been friends?"

"Since the second grade."

"And was it you or this Justin kid that was acting like a selfish coward?"

I hesitated. "Well, we both were, I guess. For different reasons."

"Be sure to tell Abby that. A girl likes it when a guy admits he's been a jerk."

"How do I tell her?" My experience, after all, wasn't in apology messages.

"Well, it might not be easy. But be sincere. Tell her what's in your heart. Can't go wrong with that. But, Quentin." She leaned in close. "Here's a hint. One rose. No carnations. A nice rose. Doesn't matter the color, with a ribbon tied around the stem. Got it?"

I nodded slowly. "I think so." For some reason I was suddenly hungry. I dug into my pizza.

She stared at me with those mom-eyes. We were quiet for a long time. Then as she looked out into the dark evening, she said, "You know, your father was quite the heartbreaker, too."

I stopped chewing. I didn't move, waiting to see if she'd go on, but half-hoping she wouldn't. I didn't want to hear how I was a chip off the ol' Chinetti block.

Mom absentmindedly bit at her fingernail. "He'd love the girls and leave them. He was handsome, and rugged, and charming, and he left a long trail of broken hearts behind him. When I caught him on my hook I knew his heartbreaking days were over. I was going to be the one to tame him, to make him settle down. But I was young. Probably too young to know what I was getting into."

"Do you wish you'd been older when you, you know, got involved with him?"

"I don't know." She was still staring off into nothing, as though trying to recall an image from somewhere in the past. "My age may have made all the difference, or it may have made none. Somehow I think—always have, still do—that we were destined to be together, him and me. But that's the funny thing about destiny. The choices people make are the only things that can screw it up. Your dad was good at making people laugh, and at screwing things up."

"How did he . . . break up with you?" I hardly

knew how to phrase the question. I knew my dad had up and left when I was six, but I'd never heard how he'd actually done it. Now that I was an expert on the art of breaking hearts, however, I was suddenly very curious.

Mom studied my face, and then looked off into the night again. "He broke my heart just like he did all the others—without looking back. One night we went out to see a movie. It was some romance. I picked it. I should have known right then—he never let me pick the movie. We held hands, and kissed. Then I woke up the next morning and he was gone. His clothes were gone, his tools were gone, half the food in the cupboards was gone. On the kitchen table was a twenty-dollar bill and a note written on a paper napkin. 'Sorry, baby, time to move on.'" Her eyes were starting to glisten in the fluorescent light of the garage bays. "Twenty dollars, and me with a six-year-old boy and no job."

We sat there digesting that bit of family history and our processed frozen pizzas.

"At least he didn't leave you a dead rat," I finally said.

Mom laughed. "Or a gift box full of dog crud," she added. And then she was really laughing. Holding her sides, hand over her mouth, snorts and gasps of raw laughter. I laughed with her, mother and son. The laughter bounced off the walls of the garage and tumbled into the parking lot. And then suddenly I saw Mom was crying, too. The tears streamed down her cheeks as the laughter went on. And for the life of me I didn't know if she was crying for happy, or crying for sad, or just plain crying.

Chapter 27

I met up with Rob the next day at lunch. He pretended not to notice me, even after I said hello. I shrugged and sat down next to him. I unwrapped my peanut butter and jelly, not minding the silence. I knew I could hold on to it longer than he could, anyway.

As I popped the last bit of crust into my mouth, Rob, still looking straight ahead, said, "I think someone at this table owes me an apology."

I looked down at the other end of the table where some kids were eating. "Yeah," I said quietly, "but you know how pig-headed Ricky can be. You might be waiting awhile."

Rob didn't look at me, but his mouth twitched as he fought down a smile.

I dug out my apple and crumpled up the empty brown paper bag. "I'm sorry, Rob. But you did get a whole box of Holey Doughs out of the deal. Even if I left you hanging, you can't complain too much about that."

Rob seemed to consider that for a moment, and then nodded and dug into his lunch. "So where were you last night?" he said with his mouth full of potato chips.

"Busy with some things."

"What kind of things?"

"Just things."

"Messenger things?"

"Yeah. More or less."

"Who was the victim this time?"

I sighed, thinking once again about what I'd done. "I don't wanna talk about it."

"Oh, come on, give me a hint. Something I can guess at."

"Not right now. Maybe later."

"Before or after you grovel at Abby's feet and beg like a dog to be forgiven for being a humongous moron?"

I turned slowly toward him. "How did you know?"

He shrugged. "I'm a man who's in the know. I got connections."

"Did you talk to Abby today?"

"Nope."

"Then how do you know what happened?"

"I talked to Abby last night."

"Oh. Where did you find her?"

Rob forced open his chocolate milk. "I didn't find her. She knocked on my door during dinner."

"Crying?"

"Her eyes were watery and her nose was red, but it might have been allergies or something."

"What did she say?"

"Oh, I think you know what she said. She told me everything. She also said she came to me because I was her best friend, and her *other* best friend didn't have much comfort to offer at the moment."

I smiled weakly, in spite of it all. "I guess that's one advantage to having two best friends."

Rob nodded. "So I invited her in for dinner with the family, and then she and I ate Holey Doughs together."

"She likes those better than chocolates anyway." I glanced over at Rob. "I'm glad you were there for her. I wasn't."

"Darn straight." Rob paused for a second, then opened his brown lunch sack and pulled out something wrapped in a paper towel. "Here, this is for you."

I unfolded it and found a Maple Fudge Holey Dough, half-smashed, but otherwise perfectly intact and gooey. "Oh, buddy. You're too awesome for words."

"I know."

I bit into the doughnut and let the sugary, fatty goodness melt in my mouth. I licked the frosting from my lips.

"You're a good friend, Rob. I'm sorry if I haven't always been one. Especially since, well, you know, since becoming the Heartbreak Messenger."

"Apology accepted," Rob said, pulling out his

ham and cheese. "But feel free to tell me again how awesome I am."

I laughed around another bite of doughnut. "Seriously. You're awesome."

"Thank you."

I sat there next to him, thinking about my successes and my failures, my business and my life. I wondered if the next apology I needed to deliver would go as smoothly. "Do you think Abby will ever speak to me again?"

"Well, I'm not a gambling man, but if I was, I'd probably put some money on it."

"Why do you say that?"

"Because she was the one that saved you the Holey Dough." Rob looked over at me and smiled big. "If it was up to me, I'd have eaten it myself."

Chapter 28

I left our apartment early the next morning, wanting to be at the front door of Pretty Bouquets right when they opened at ten o'clock. There were hearts to fix and a friendship to patch and a schedule to keep. There was also still some thinking to do.

I rode my bike along a meandering road on the far west side of town. A dusty cloud trailed in my wake. I swerved in and out, making patterns in the dirt. I passed the Bus Barn, where the yellow school buses were lined up in a neat row, resting for the weekend. Up ahead, warehouses and self-storage complexes sat back in the trees on the left, while a small stream ran through a gully on the right. Eventually the road would go past the backside of Lincoln Hill Park and let out near the flower shop. The long route gave me time to think.

I'd rehearsed about twenty different speeches for Abby in front of the bathroom mirror, but none of them seemed right. Apologies are never easy, I guess. And apparently the bigger the bonehead you've been, the more they hurt coming up. Mom had told me to say what was in my heart. There was plenty in there—assuming I could get it all out.

To be completely honest, the biggest problem was trying to figure out my own feelings. Everything just seemed so complicated.

Abby. Me. Justin. Friend. Buddy. Best friend. Girlfriend. A few weeks ago, I'd thought I knew what all of those words meant. Then somehow everything had become muddled and twisted and blurred. Part of me wished that things could get back to normal, uncomplicated. But at the same time, I wasn't so sure that's what I wanted at all.

Maybe it wasn't that I needed a Rosetta Stone for girls. Maybe I needed one to figure out myself.

Engine noise rumbled into my thoughts.

At first I figured it was one of the school buses out for a weekend spin. But it was the wrong kind of rumble. It was smaller, vaguely familiar—and it pushed needles of fear into my skin.

Ten yards ahead, a motorcycle pulled out from one of the side roads that led back into the complex of warehouses. The rider wore a white T-shirt and a black leather jacket. He looked up the road, ready to make a left turn in the direction I was headed. Then he glanced my way.

Gunner peered over the top of his sunglasses and smiled.

My life flashed before my eyes. It was boring and short and about to end way too early. But the thought that rose above all others was, *Why today?*

I glanced around, but there was nowhere my bike could go where the motorcycle couldn't follow. I slammed on my brakes.

Gunner's motorcycle shot toward me with a roar. Within seconds his front tire bumped up against mine and his headlight filled my vision.

I took a deep breath. Perhaps he just wanted to

talk. Maybe he didn't know about the black book betrayal with his ex-girlfriends.

He let his bike idle to a monotonous growl. "Hey, Sly," he said with a smile. "I was just heading out to see what pain I could cause. Nice of you to stop by."

Hmmm. He probably knows. "Hey, Gunner. Um, I gotta go. Someone's waiting for me."

Gunner flicked his handlebar and the Beast lurched forward, giving my bike a violent nudge. I scooted back, my toes on the ground to keep my balance. Gunner kept rolling slowly forward as I tried to increase the gap between our tires.

"You know," he said over the noise of the Kawasaki, "my life has really sucked lately. It took some time, Sly, but I finally figured out what to blame it on."

I glanced behind me. "Rotten luck?"

"Nope. Some kid I hired to do a simple job. Turns out he had a death wish."

I tightened my grip on the handlebars and tried to keep my voice steady. "Listen, Gunner, I . . . I did what you asked. I broke up with the girls and didn't tell them about each other." There was now several feet between our tires.

Gunner's smile turned into a sneer. "Nice try, Sly. But I want my money back. And I'll take it, right after I beat the . . ."

I slammed my pedals forward with everything I had. I swerved hard, scraping past the Beast and ducking as Gunner's hand shot out to grab me. I heard him curse and then the engine roared to life like a war machine.

My mind raced. I couldn't outpace Gunner when he was sitting on 120 horsepower. There was no chance of a cop car passing by out here. And natural disasters never strike when and where you need them. My only hope was to hold out until I reached some public place where Gunner couldn't beat me to death without witnesses.

The air vibrated as the motorcycle pulled up alongside me. Gunner smiled his jungle cat grin as his hair danced around his face. He pushed his sunglasses up on his nose and then swerved toward me in one smooth motion.

I frantically pulled my handlebars to the right

and then yanked back, inches away from slipping into the gully on the side of the road.

Gunner laughed. He was like a cat playing with the mouse before devouring it whole. He edged his motorcycle closer as I pedaled on the stony lip of the gully. I glanced down to see a thin line of water trickling at the bottom. The gully was less than two yards across, but it was shoulder-deep with steep walls. If I fell, I probably wouldn't break anything, but the only escape would be through Gunner's fists.

Something smacked the backside of my head. I looked over in time to see Gunner reach over and slap my head again.

"What's the matter, Sly?" he shouted. "I thought the Heartbreaker wanted to play tough with Gunner. Well, you ain't seen nothing yet."

Twenty yards ahead the road pulled to the left. My heart sank. I knew what Gunner was going to do. He would crowd me out as we came around that curve, and I'd go crashing into the gully.

My body urged me to hit the brakes, to turn around and try to find help in the warehouses half a mile back. But it was Saturday—no one would be there.

We were almost at the curve. Gunner saw my wide eyes, my look of panic. He laughed.

I was ready to slam on the brakes when I saw a large round stone in my path just where the gully wall plunged downward and the curve in the road pulled to the left. Knowing that broken limbs were probably a sure thing at that point, I poured on the last bit of speed my legs could give me.

My front tire hit the smooth side of the stone, which was slanted just enough to give me the lift I needed. I flew into the air over the gully. I had the speed. I had the height. I had the momentum. I felt like throwing my arms into the air and shouting, "Free at last!"

I'd taken enough bike jumps to know how to position my legs, grip the handlebars, and keep everything steady on impact. Not that I was ever very good at it. As my rear tire crashed into the ground on the other side of the gully, my angle was all wrong. The bike slipped out from under me and sent me tumbling into the trees.

I scrambled to my feet, feeling every scrape and bruise along my body. Nothing seemed to be broken, which almost made me smile. Down the dirt road, Gunner was turning around as quickly as he could. I grabbed the handlebars of my bike, but saw that the back rim looked like a wavy letter *D* with whiskers made out of spokes.

Gunner wasn't likely to risk his motorcycle trying that jump, but I wasn't going to wait to find out. Legs still wobbling, I pushed my bike through the trees.

The ground gradually sloped upward. My calves burned with each step. I caught a branch underfoot and slid back a few yards. I kinda knew where I was, but really had no idea where the trees would end and civilization begin. I stopped for a moment to catch my breath, hands on knees.

I have to hurry. I have to keep going. I couldn't let Abby down again.

And then I heard that familiar rumble, faint but distinct. The Beast was on the move.

I couldn't tell which direction the sound came from—in front or behind. I ran, pushing my wounded bike through the sycamores and poplars. Moments later I burst through the edge of the trees and landed on an expanse of trimmed green grass.

I was in Lincoln Hill Park. In the distance I saw the path up to the top of the hill, and then the parking lot beyond where I'd first met Gunner. I briefly wondered if Gunner appreciated the irony of that as I turned and saw him bearing down on me across the green grass. I dropped my bike and ran for it. I headed toward the neighborhoods beyond the park, where the masses of civilized people were picking up their morning papers.

But Gunner was in control again. He curved around and cut me off. I turned and he cut me off again. I rounded the corner of a brick maintenance shed, hoping it would at least separate me from Gunner's view. But the edge of the shed was met by a chain-link fence, creating the perfect corner for catching a mouse.

Gunner parked his motorcycle in front of me and slid off with a swagger.

My legs were Jell-O and my lungs were burning.

Trapped between wall and fence, I knew if I ran I wouldn't make it ten feet before he tackled me. I stood as straight as I could and stared at my pitiful reflection in his sunglasses.

He pulled off his black leather jacket and draped it across the seat of the Beast. He slid the shades from his face to reveal steely eyes that focused on me like machine gun sights. He stretched his arms back and rolled his head around, like he was getting ready to box at the gym. "All right, Sly. Time to do business."

I prepared myself for death or unconsciousness, whichever came first. But as I closed my eyes, Abby's face was the only thing that came to mind.

Gunner took a step forward and raised his fist.

"Gunner!"

My eyes popped open and Gunner spun around. Past him, down the park path and over the grass, I saw ten hulking forms in gray shorts and crimson T-shirts bounding toward us in single file. Duke Ripling trotted at the front of the line.

"Gunner!" Duke shouted again. As they approached, Duke called out a command and pointed his fingers to the sides. The John P. Westmore defensive line split in two and formed a half circle around me and Gunner before coming to a stop.

Duke stepped up to Gunner.

"What do you want, Ripling?" Gunner's shoulders were back and his head up, but he was still six inches shorter than Duke.

"What you doing with my little man here?" Duke asked.

"Nothing I need you around for."

Duke squared his shoulders. "Maybe you oughta pick on someone your own size."

I couldn't believe my luck. I restrained myself from launching into some sort of *Go team!* cheerleader chant.

"Oh, you're a real hero, aren't you?" Gunner said the words with bravado, but his eyes jumped for a split second to the football players surrounding us. He glanced back toward his jacket and I remembered the knife.

A step forward put Duke inches from Gunner's face. "I don't think you understand. The little messenger man is with me. Anything happens to him, I'm going to take it personal, and I'll probably get just a little angry. You do know why they call me Duke the Ripper, don't you?"

I'd wondered that myself and wished he would go into detail for Gunner's sake.

Gunner sidled toward his bike, throwing on his jacket as he tossed a leg over the Beast. "Shove a jockstrap in it, Ripling."

Duke lunged forward and Gunner jumped, trying to push his motorcycle along while hitting the ignition. It finally turned and the defensive line let him pass with a few taunts and insults. Gunner revved the engine and took off across the grass.

Laughing, Duke turned back to me and held up his hand for a high-five. "Righteous, little messenger." I hit his hand hard, and then wished I hadn't.

"Take five, guys," Duke said to his teammates. Half of the players collapsed to the ground, while the others trotted over to the drinking fountain.

It took a moment for my heart to slow down enough for me to talk. "Thanks, Duke. Sir. I really appreciate that."

"No worries, man. Like I told you the other

day, I think you're all right. Now that Gunner knows I got your back, he won't even look your way. He's all leather and steel on the outside, but I've never seen such a cream puff."

"Well, thanks." I stood there for a moment, wondering what else I could say. I felt like hugging the guy, since he'd just saved my skin and all, but I was afraid that might not go over too well, especially in front of the team. Instead I said, "So, hey, have you talked to Lisa lately?"

Duke's face fell and he sighed. Perhaps not the best question to ask, but at least he didn't start crying. "I've tried. I even sat outside her window all night long on Wednesday, at least until her grandma chased me away with a fire poker. She just won't listen. Won't even talk to me."

"I'm sorry to hear that." Once again, I had the feeling Lisa was missing out on something, that they were both suffering for no good reason.

"If there was just a way to make her understand," Duke said.

Right then an idea popped into my head and snapped into place, like magnetic puzzle pieces finding each other at last. "Hey, Duke . . . there's something I want to talk over with you. I need to think it through first, and I'm late for an appointment right now, but I might be able to return the favor."

His eyebrows scrunched together. "Uh, sure, man, stop by the house any time and we'll talk."

"Okay," I said as I headed off to grab my bike, my mind already whirling with ideas that hopefully wouldn't get me pulverized or threatened or make me feel guilty. Maybe. "And thanks again."

Chapter 29

This time when I walked into the Pretty Bouquets flower shop, the lady behind the counter shook her head sadly. "I'm sorry, dear, but there was a funeral this morning. I'm all out of carnations."

"That's okay. I'm actually here for something different."

That made her eyebrows lift just a little.

"I need a rose. A really nice rose. It's for a friend. She's a girl. She's just a friend—my best friend, really—but, you know, maybe later on down the road . . . anyway. I need to apologize. I need to let her know I'm still here for her. As a friend."

The woman gave a nod of satisfaction. "Now *that's* something I can help you with."

She turned behind her and opened a glass door. The cold air flooded into the small store. She gestured to a collection of roses on the far right-hand side. "Now, a short-stemmed rose is something you want to avoid. It's what one gives his mother on Mother's Day. And they're usually cheap enough to buy at the grocery store, which is always a *faux pas*."

"A phoo-what?"

But the lady was deep into her floral consultation. "No, what you need is a long-stemmed rose. These are usually fuller and larger than an average short-stemmed, and often last longer once they bloom. This allows the recipient more time to think about your kindness and devotion." She moved over to the large buckets of roses on the left. "Always select a rose with a number of leaves still attached, as this suggests authenticity. As for color, in your situation, you may want to avoid red, since it tends to be indicative of romantic love. But a yellow rose is a sign of friendship, a white rose a sign of peace . . ."

She moved toward the display of long-stemmed roses and carefully pulled one out. "In your particular situation, I have a good feeling about this one here." The rose was a deep lavender, with darker purple peeking out at the edges of the petals just starting to open up. Even to me it looked pretty cool.

"Can I get it plain like that, with a ribbon tied around the stem?" I asked.

She cocked her head to one side. "A very refined choice. But don't you want to know how much it costs first?"

"No. I'll take it."

Chapter 30

I arrived at Mick's when the sun was just high enough to cast shadows over the picnic table. Abby sat there with Rob, just as he had promised me she would. As I headed through the parking lot, I glanced over at the garage where Mom was working on a Dodge Neon (spark plugs). She saw the rose in my hand and gave me a quick wink.

I stopped just short of the picnic table. Abby studied a page in her spiral notebook, a pencil in her hand. She didn't look at me. A five-gallon bucket of walnuts was on the ground next to Rob, a Tupperware on the table, and a metal nutcracker in his hand. He raised the nutcracker in greeting.

"Hey, Quentin." He nodded toward Abby and gave me a thumbs-up.

"Thanks, Rob," I said.

"No problem." He put a nut in the cracker and snapped it open.

I stared at him for a moment. "Rob," I finally said.

"Oh. Oh, right. I, um, I'm going to go help your mom, uh, hold wrenches or something." He tossed down the nutcracker and left.

I cleared my throat. "Abby, what I have to say . . ."

"Sit down, Mr. Chinetti."

I immediately knew what kind of conversation this was going to be.

I sat down across the table from Abby and laid the rose right in front of me where it couldn't be missed.

"I have three questions for you." Abby wrote in her notebook as she spoke. "If you can answer those three questions honestly, then there's a good chance I can find it in my heart to forgive you."

Oh, boy, here we go.

She looked up and locked eyes with me, then

raised her left index finger. "What were you doing on Monday afternoon when you stood me up for our homework session?"

I absentmindedly picked up the nutcracker and turned it over in my hands. "Well, I told you that Rob and I were out at the scrap yard."

Abby's eyes narrowed, and I knew this was no time to fool around. I grabbed a walnut.

"I was there doing a Heartbreak Messenger job." *Crack.*

"You admit that you left me hanging so that you could break a poor girl's heart and earn a few bucks?

"Is that one of the three questions?"

"Don't question my questions, Mr. Chinetti."

I pulled the walnut meat out and tossed it into the Tupperware. "Actually, it was a guy."

"Who was?"

"The person I delivered the message to on Monday. It was a guy, not a girl."

"Oh. Really?" Abby's district attorney mask dropped for a split second before popping back into place. "That doesn't make a difference. Why did you lie to me about it the other night?"

I raised an argumentative finger in protest. "I didn't lie. Everything I said was true."

"Don't give me that, *Messenger*. You used words to send the message you wanted me to hear. And you didn't want me to hear the truth."

There was no way around logic like that. I nodded slowly and grabbed another walnut. "You're right. I'm sorry. But you said if I'd been doing a Messenger job, that you wouldn't speak to me until next Presidents' Day." I gave her a tiny grin. "And that's a long ways off."

She stared at me for a moment and then looked away, but not before I saw a smile dance through her eyes. "Okay." She placed a checkmark next to something in her notebook and then studied the page for a moment. When she looked up, her eyes were hard once more. She raised a second finger. "Why did you agree to Justin's job? Why did you break up with me for him?"

I took a deep breath. I'd actually rehearsed an answer for this one. But Abby's picnic table interrogation made me stop and think a little harder. She wanted me to be as honest as possible. I owed her that much.

I slowly moved the walnut through my fingers. "Well, the best answer is that I was being selfish. I needed the money and Justin was willing to pay . . ."

Abby's eyes grew wide.

"But that's not the only way I was being selfish," I quickly added. "I guess I was thinking a lot more about my own feelings than about yours." *Crack.*

The hard lines on Abby's face softened. "What feelings?"

"Well, I've never really liked Justin. I kept trying to convince myself that it was because he's so . . . Justin. But I think maybe it was something else all along. I think I was jealous of him. All I could see was him stealing away my best friend, you know? I wanted you back. So when the opportunity came, I took it." I loaded the metal cracker with another walnut.

"So you were jealous of Justin. Because you missed me as a *friend*." It was both a statement and a question, with a force behind it as gentle as a hemi-head engine.

Weeks before, I might have missed what she

was saying entirely. I would have taken what she said at face value and replied, "Yep." But now, I could feel the mental tumblers fall into place as a lock snapped open in my mind. It wasn't a Rosetta Stone, but it did give me a tiny glimmer of insight into what her message really meant.

And I knew what I said next had to be completely honest. No movie script, no one-liners. From the heart.

"Kinda. That was only part of it. There's also something else that's a little more complicated and it took me awhile to figure it out."

"What?" She almost whispered the word.

My whole body itched. The walnut slipped and hit the table with a hollow smack.

"I've tried to tell myself that I wasn't jealous you were his girlfriend, just that I missed having you around. Missed hanging out with you, seeing you everyday, just being there. And I did miss that. But . . . I *was* jealous that you were his girlfriend, too."

"Why?" This time it was definitely a whisper.

I picked up the walnut again. My hand shook just a little. I took a deep breath. *Be honest.*

"I like you, Abby. A lot. That's probably the biggest reason I had problems with Justin."

Abby looked at me across the table, but my eyes kept slipping away from hers. "How long have you known?" she asked.

I looked at my watch. "Consciously? Probably about forty seconds. But a lot longer than that, you know, underneath." *Crack*.

I risked a glance her way. She seemed to be holding back a smile. No, a whole river of smiles. The dimple in her left cheek was getting deeper.

I plunged ahead. "But, Abby, the problem is . . . well, I don't think I'm ready to do anything about it."

Abby's eyebrows furrowed, bringing a dam down in front of the river. "What do you mean? How can you like somebody—a lot—and not be ready to do anything about it?"

"Mostly, I guess I feel like I'm too young to have a girlfriend."

"Too young? Quentin, we're thirteen years old. In a few years we'll be practically almost adults. What's too young about that?"

"Just what you said. Someday we'll be adults,

but not right now. Right now we're kids. Kids hang out and have fun. And that's what I want to do. I feel like if we start dating now, it'll just be another game."

"Are you saying my feelings are just part of a game?" Abby raised her voice. This was not going according to plan. Heck, I had lost track of any plan a few miles back.

"No, Abby, that's not what I'm saying. I mean . . . well, what do you want a boyfriend for?"

She paused for a moment. "I don't just want a boyfriend. I want to be with someone because I like them. I guess." She looked hard into my eyes. "But it's not a game. It's serious. When you— Justin, whoever—broke up with me, it hurt. A lot. And that was real."

I stared back, trying to understand the storm of feelings inside of me and explain them at the same time. It was like reading a newspaper caught in a whirlwind. "You're right. It *was* real. And it *is* serious. I didn't see that when I started doing the Heartbreak Messenger thing. I watched a lot of people who thought that love was about class rings, or about little black books, or being seen by everyone, or getting what they wanted. But that's not what love's about. It's not a game. If you treat it that way, people get hurt and . . ." I choked up, something catching in my throat that I had to cough past. "You shouldn't fool around with love, you know. It's a commitment, to be together in something permanent. To take care of each other and stick together, no matter what."

My eyes were watering for no logical reason, except perhaps that I had delivered a message so meaningful to me that it hovered just outside of my ability to understand, but not my ability to feel.

"And I don't know about you," I said as I wiped at my eyes. "But I'm not ready for that much responsibility yet."

If I had just been sitting in front of a girl that I liked—a lot—then I probably would have felt like a complete dweeb. But as it was, I sat in front of my best friend. Abby dropped her counting hand and placed it on top of mine, sending a comforting, static warmth through my body.

"How old were you when your dad left?" she asked. Her eyes were softer now. "Five?"

"Six."

"Do you think he loved your mom?"

I glanced briefly over toward the garage bay and sniffled. "Maybe in his own way. But for him it was a game."

Abby nodded. We both knew she was right. And that I was right, too. Somehow, we were both right together.

After forever, she lifted her hand from mine and picked up the nutcracker and a walnut. "You know, after Rob and I ate too many Holey Doughs the other night, I went over to Justin's house to force him to talk to me."

"Seriously?"

"Does that really surprise you?"

I shook my head. "No, I guess not. Blunder-bangs probably didn't expect to see you, though. He doesn't know you like I do."

"No. I don't think he did. I think he expected me to just take a message and be done with it. But I wanted to hear him say it. I wanted him to treat me with the respect I deserve, I guess. So I asked him three questions."

"And?"

Crack. "He couldn't answer them honestly."

"Oh. What a punk."

Abby giggled. "Yeah. What a punk." She picked the meat out of the shell and tossed it into the Tupperware.

"So . . ." I said. "You only asked me two questions. Is there another?"

She shook her head. "No. You already answered it."

"Hey, Abby?" I said.

"Yeah?"

I picked up the rose and handed it to her across the table. "Is it all right if I ask you out sometime? Like maybe when I'm sixteen?"

"Sixteen!? Sheesh, Quentin, we'll be ancient by then. How about fifteen?"

"Fifteen and a half."

"Deal." She brought the rose up to her face. "Really?"

"Oh, I'll be around," she said with a smile. "But that doesn't mean you won't have to chase me." She hopped up and headed toward the garage. "Hey, Rob and I are riding bikes out to the river. You coming?"

"Of course," I said as I caught up to her. "Or . . . how about we hike the trails instead? My bike had a minor fender bender."

"Okay."

"By the way, there's something else I meant to tell you."

Abby gave me a worried look. "What? I'm not sure I can handle many more of your messages this week."

"Just that I'm done being the Heartbreak Messenger. I'm giving it up."

"Really? About time."

"Yeah, I know when to call it quits." I smiled to myself. The Heartbreak Messenger had retired, but that just meant I'd have more time for other . . . business plans. "Besides, I've got something even better in mind."

Thank you for reading this FEIWEL AND FRIENDS book.
The Friends who made

The Heartbreak Messenger

possible are:

Jean Feiwel, Publisher

Liz Szabla, Editor in Chief

Rich Deas, Creative Director

Holly West, Associate Editor

Dave Barrett, Executive Managing Editor

Nicole Liebowitz Moulaison, Production Manager

Lauren A. Burniac, Editor

Anna Roberto, Assistant Editor

FIND OUT MORE ABOUT OUR AUTHORS AND ARTISTS
AND OUR FUTURE PUBLISHING AT
MACKIDS.COM.

OUR BOOKS ARE FRIENDS FOR LIFE